MAKAI KING

TARA FAIRFIELD

MAKAI SERIES NOVEL #2

Creative Force Press

Creative Force Press

Makai King
Makai Series
© 2014 by Tara Fairfield

This title is also available as an eBook. Visit
www.CreativeForcePress.com/titles for more information.

Published by Creative Force Press
4704 Pacific Ave, Suite C, Lacey, WA 98503
www.CreativeForcePress.com

ISBN: 978-1-939989-12-3

Printed in the United States of America
Cover design by www.IRCprintanddesign.com

DEDICATION

In memory of my dad, James J. Fairfield, who instilled in me a love of the ocean and encouraged me to follow my dreams. This one's for you dad.

For Griffin and Granger who are my fierce heroes and Adelaide who spreads joy wherever she goes and will always be my sweet princess!

PROLOGUE

When my friends in Moku-ola first informed me my destiny included being their queen, I thought they were crazy. But now, I've gotten used to the idea and enjoy life under the sea. Sure, problems come at me faster than a seagull can steal your lunch, but whose life doesn't have issues? At least as queen I can do something. I have the power to get up and take action.

Since being crowned queen of Moku-ola last year, my life has been amazing. My sister and I are friends again, I get to hang out with a guy who treats me like I'm the most special person in the world, and best of all, I have a Creator who loves me. He has gifted me with the ability to speak to all sea life from anywhere I am. How lucky am I!

Things would be almost perfect if only my boyfriend's brother wasn't a crazed lunatic who controlled the sharks. Oh, and if we could also figure out what to do with a megalodon shark we've trapped in a chasm (I call him Donnie). Anyway, I haven't lost hope his brother might be saved. Somehow, I'm gonna figure out how to reach him. Hopefully, that won't entail anyone I care about getting attacked by his sharks. Been there, done that.

CHAPTER 1

HO'OMANA'O'ANA

MEMORY

"Wake up, Tessa, wake up."

I peered at the blurry image of Akalei hovering above me, sure it couldn't be morning already. Sheets tangled around my legs and a slight pounding behind my eyes reminded me I hadn't slept well which was no surprise given the events of the past week.

"Okay, I'm awake. Give me a minute and I'll meet you in the tunnel." Rubbing my eyes, I kicked off the sheets.

"Hurry, Sid reports hundreds of fish have washed up on Maui. Surface dwellers are already investigating and who knows what evidence they've destroyed."

Heat flushed my cheeks. "This has Moho written all over it, he's got to be involved somehow. Hopefully we can figure out what's killing our fish before any more perish."

She spun on her heels, flipping long, braided hair over her shoulder. "Don't take too long. We have lots of ground to cover, and

I want to make it back for dinner with my sweetie."

Waving her off, I dragged myself out of bed, tucked my hair into a ponytail and shrugged off the last vestiges of sleep. Tugging my favorite yellow shorts on over my bathing suit, I tiptoed over the moat and out the door, inhaling deeply and throwing back my shoulders, determined to concentrate on problems I could do something about, like protecting those within my realm.

Lizzy's cold nose greeted me, nudging against my thigh and spreading goosebumps along my skin. I stroked her head, and traipsed out the family entrance. My faithful sea lion never wandered far from my side, taking her role as ambassador very seriously.

Akalei waited at the door, tapping her foot impatiently. She sported a sleeveless purple wetsuit embellished with glittering silver swirls flowing up her side. Style came easily to Akalei. No matter the occasion, she sparkled. Her smile lifted my mood.

She bumped my shoulder as we strolled through the lava tunnel towards the water. "Love ya, *tita*."

Warmth curled around my heart as I bumped her back. "Thanks for coming along. I know Kele wasn't thrilled about you joining me."

She shrugged. "He's far too protective. It'll do him good. Besides, he's just grumpy he's not coming with us. You know how much he likes visiting the surface. So, what's the plan?"

"We need clues, let's hope the scene of this crime coughs some up. Sid says people on the surface are also checking this out, so we'll have to be careful. Maybe we'll even try some undercover work." I winked at her.

She laughed, "Kele will be soooo jealous."

I inhaled the now familiar sweet musty air of the tunnels leading from our family entrance to the makai. Stretching my arms into the air I jogged toward the ocean, and Akalei followed close behind. A soft glow radiated through the volcanic walls, casting muted light and shadows across our path. My muscles warmed and lengthened with each stride. When we arrived where the sea lapped against our shore, Lizzy barked and dove in, spraying chilly water against our legs. She had her own protection issues and always liked to check out the area before I entered.

I paused, pointing my finger at Akalei with a look of warning. "Don't try anything crazy. I don't want to face Kele if something happens to you. Not again."

She rolled her eyes and leapt into the water. Laughing, I plunged after her, relishing the rush of sea flowing across my skin, caressing and welcoming me.

Humpback whales clicked greetings at us, their song resonating through the ocean like a symphony. Gurgling, throaty squeals combined with higher-pitched siren calls amplified through the ocean's microphone, sending chills of delight spinning down my spine. New life burst forth everywhere. We took a detour to say hello to my favorite mother and baby humpback. Little Elmo weighed over a ton already at just a few weeks old. Dancing gracefully through the water, he and his mother pursued us a few miles as we tracked around the Maui coastline, their bodies gliding, spinning around one another in a choreographed ballet. Exhilaration coursed through my veins as I joined their dance. Whenever we broke the surface, Elmo slapped his fins, splashing me with water, much to Lizzy's dismay. She darted in between us to ensure I kept a proper distance to avoid being accidentally crushed by his playfulness.

When we finally reached Sid, his tentacles bunched up around his body in frustration. Octopi don't appreciate being kept waiting, and Sid demonstrated less patience than most. He informed us a crowd had gathered on the beach to check out the dead fish, and directed us to the area.

Akalei and I crawled onto the sand, careful to blend into the crowd. Dead bodies littered the beach, reeking of rotting fish and gagging us both. I forced back a retching episode and even with my hands covering my mouth the putrid stench of death nauseated me. Stooping over the closest pile to examine it more closely for clues, no outward signs of trauma were evident on the fish. Akalei snatched a couple, holding them as far from her body as possible, and dropped them in her bag for Kele to examine later. We strode along the beach towards a crowd of people gathered, hoping to learn more about what the surface dwellers knew regarding the mass deaths. Two marine biologists in uniforms stood at the center of the crowd. We hung back and listened, ears tuned for possible leads.

"It may take us a while to figure out what happened. We need everyone to leave the beach. This area will be quarantined."

I glanced at Akalei. This wasn't good news. One of the older men in the crowd stalked toward the parking lot, catching my attention. Dressed in a white shirt and trousers, he didn't quite fit in with the rest of the crowd. I motioned to Akalei and we followed him. When he slid into his BMW, I recognized him as Henry; the treasure hunter working with Moho. He hid his hair under a baseball cap but his swagger was unmistakable. What was he doing here?

Akalei grabbed my arm and yanked me behind a truck, scraping my leg against its fender.

"Ouch, why'd you do that?" I hopped on one foot, holding my hand against the cut to keep it from bleeding.

She pointed across the parking lot and whispered, "He's not the only problem we have."

I peeked around the truck as Moho leapt onto a shiny motorcycle and sped after the BMW, his face a hard, blank mask.

"Great, just great," I mumbled under my breath. Since when did Moho hang out on the surface? And where did he get a motorcycle?

"What do we do now?" Akalei asked.

I turned and marched down the beach where Lizzy waited. "Give me the bag." I thrust my open hand to Akalei, and she handed me the pouch crammed with dead fish. "Lizzy, deliver this to Kele and Kupua. It would be great if Kele could figure out how these fish died. Tell Kupua we're remaining on land to investigate what few clues we've uncovered."

Akalei frowned at me. "Kupua needs to know we spotted Moho."

"I'll tell him as soon as we return to Moku-ola. If we say

11

something now, he'll get all protective and probably come to the surface and track us down. Right now, our best chance is to maintain a low profile and discover what we can about how Moho and Henry are connected to these dead fish. We're just collecting clues, no danger."

She glared at me but didn't argue.

Lizzy shook her head. She didn't like leaving us alone.

I shoved the bag of fish in her mouth. "You can return once you've delivered this package, if it makes you feel better."

She dropped the bag and barked.

I shook my finger at her. "That's an order."

She whined, but yanked the bag and sulked into the surf, her head drooping.

Akalei patted my shoulder. "You're gonna pay for that later."

As surf rolled back and forth across my feet I watched her disappear beneath the waves and hoped her feelings were all I'd have to worry about. Kupua wasn't going be happy when we didn't come back as expected. Shoving worry aside, I rinsed the fish smell off my hands and pivoted to face Akalei. "Time for undercover work."

CHAPTER 2

PILIALOHA

FRIENDSHIP

Kahului buzzed with information about Henry, the elusive, wealthy treasure hunter, renting out a large section of a resort in Wailea. Akalei and I hitched a ride in the back of a farm truck headed across the island. Not exactly a fly ride, but we weren't in a position to be picky.

Akalei bounced into the truck and perched with her legs hanging off the back, waving at cars passing by, her long braid thrown over her shoulder, loose wisps of hair flying in the wind. She patted the spot next to her, beaming. "Tessa, come sit. Enjoy yourself."

I rolled my eyes, but plopped next to her anyway, her infectious mood inching into my spirit. "Aren't you concerned Moho and Henry are using a new weapon to kill the fish? If we don't figure out what's going on, more of our friends could die."

"Of course I'm concerned, but I've learned worrying about

something doesn't make it go away or help fix it. We aren't supposed to worry, Tessa. We're supposed to do what we can and trust the Creator with the rest."

"Harder than it sounds." I sighed and tilted my head into the wind, relishing the breeze tickling my cheeks. My ponytail whipped in all directions, tugging against the tie holding it in place. I reached to secure it and bumped Akalei's shoulder. "Thanks for being such a great *hoaloha*, *lei*. Don't know what I'd do without you."

She laughed and craned her head back, closing her eyes as the sun beat down on her face, setting her skin aglow. Even in the back of a dumpy truck, surrounded by crates of pineapples and assorted tools, she shined.

"What was it like, Akalei, growing up under the sea with Moho and Kupua?"

She straightened and her smile faded. "We were all close to Moho once, best of friends. My father served as a member of the royal guard, so I lived in the palace as a child. My mother died giving birth to me, so Kele, Moho and Kupua became my family. Growing up, we pretty much had free rein to explore as we pleased. The ocean served as our playground, and every waking moment we spent learning its secrets. Our people have a saying: *Children of the sea joined together in friendship become a blessing to all.* I thought they wrote the phrase just for us, until the world shifted and Moho lost it."

"What happened to your father?"

She looked down and picked at her nails. "He died a few

14

years ago in an accident. He was cutting turtles free of fishing lines and didn't realize how close a boat had come before it was too late and the propellers hit him. It happened fast, so he didn't suffer."

Pain stung my heart. I placed my arm around her. "I'm sorry. I know what it's like to lose a parent."

She nudged me. "I know. It all happened a long time ago. I grab every second I can with those I love and don't want to waste any chance to make another good memory."

A car passed by, honking as a blond-haired surfer-type guy hung out the window and waved at us, shouting something lost in the wind.

I laughed. "You mean like this awesome good time we're having right now?"

She beamed. "Exactly."

"Do you think there's hope for Moho? Can he be saved?"

"I don't know, but I agree we have to try. None of us want to give up on him, even Kele, despite his grumbling. Deep down, both Kele and Kupua feel responsible for not doing more the day Moho discovered his gift with the sharks."

Kupua had shared the story with me when we'd first met. Moho's anger triggered the sharks, but he didn't know how to gain control, killing one of their friends as a result. Moho never returned to Moku-ola, suffering guilt, anger and bitterness. I tried to imagine what it would feel like if Rachel suddenly refused to be part of my family and shuddered, knowing it would leave a big, gaping hole. Nothing would convince me to stop hoping for her return. My heart wrenched for the torment Kupua must have experienced as he witnessed his brother fill with anger and hate.

When we reached Wailea, we hopped off the truck and waved our thanks to the driver, sprinting across the road toward the ocean. The driver, an older Hawaiian man with soft eyes and a crooked smile, nodded and continued his journey. No one really gave us much notice, just two young women walking around Maui on a warm sunny day, headed for the beach. We blended right in.

One of the great things about Maui is the mix of people you find on the street at any given moment. Old, young, rich, poor, families, former hippies, surfers, locals and tourists all melded together in the ease of the aloha spirit. The beach was a great equalizer, creating friends among the most unlikely characters. So, of course, no one bothered to give a second glance to us, even if one wore a purple wetsuit and looked like a goddess. Well, maybe a few surfers took a second glance, but not because they had any suspicions we were undercover from a city beneath the sea. Akalei flashed a smile at me, oblivious to the attention she evoked, and I inhaled the warm ocean air, grateful to share such a beautiful day with my friend, even if we weren't here to relax.

The resort driveway bordered a golf course dotted with palm trees swaying in the trade winds. We stopped at the concierge desk, flashing smiles at the young man sitting by the phone arranging brochures and looking helpful. His Hawaiian shirt blazed with blue, green, yellow, and orange flowers which threatened to put the most avid tourist to shame. Around his neck hung several leis, slightly covering a name tag suggesting his name was either Don or Jon, I couldn't tell which. He exuded the traditional aloha grin and helpful attitude of resort staff everywhere.

I leaned against his desk, absently stroking one of the many brochures on fun activities available on Maui. "Hey. Our uncle Henry asked us to come pick him up. He's in one of those fancy villas. Can you tell us which one? I lost the number and don't want him to get mad."

"Of course, ladies, happy to help." He typed something on his computer. "Are you enjoying the island?"

"What's not to love? The water here is amazing!"

He nodded and smiled as his eyes scanned me. His body shifted, moving closer into my personal space. "Your uncle's in Villa 6." He whipped out a map of the resort and drew us a path indicating how to find Henry.

I plucked the map from his hand and winked, leaning away to put more space between us. "Thank you, you've been very helpful. I'll be sure to let your manager know."

Akalei tugged on my arm as he about tripped over himself thanking me. She giggled. "Keep smiling at him and he's going to climb over the desk."

"I doubt it. I just didn't want him asking too many questions."

She clucked her tongue at me. "Tessa, you don't realize your own beauty. You radiate from the inside out, like a true queen."

Heat rose in my cheeks. "Stop it, we have work to do."

She laughed and squeezed my shoulder.

We followed the path Don or Jon, I still wasn't sure, mapped out for us to Henry's section. Surprisingly, I didn't see much in the way of security. Tropical flowers covered the grounds, shaded by Koa trees, creating cool, lush walkways, chilling my skin after the sunny ride in the truck. Gardenia and plumeria scented the air, spreading a sweet, fresh, floral fragrance. A sigh escaped me and momentary longing of life above surface whispered across my senses.

Warning messages flashed from somewhere close by, startling me back to reality. Looking around, I spotted a plump black-footed albatross, one of the largest birds in the islands, perched in a tree above our heads. She gazed down at me and blinked, introducing herself as Maxie, and warning me Moho was on the beach with Henry just around the corner.

I retreated a few steps and thanked her, glancing over at Akalei and putting a finger to my mouth for quiet.

She whispered, "Did that bird just talk to you?" I nodded, and her eyes widened. "Wow, Tessa, what can't you do?"

I guided us back around the other side of the cabana, crouching low and slinking like fugitives on the run. I wanted some distance between us and Moho, but not so much we couldn't hear what they were saying. Maxie flew past and swooped onto the beach a few inches from where Moho sat. He frowned at her. She skittered back a few feet as he lifted his leg and kicked sand in her direction. She hopped around a few minutes and settled in again, nestling into the sand. He turned his attention back to Henry, who lay relaxing in a hammock holding one of those fancy drinks with an umbrella.

Henry spoke, gesturing with his free hand. "You haven't lived up to your end of the bargain. I practically handed your enemies to you, and still I have nothing."

Moho grunted. "You allowed them to kidnap you and defeat our great shark. You handed me nothing. Now they know about the flute."

"They know nothing," Henry chuckled. "None of them have any idea what the flute can do, or how to play it. Besides, it's not our only weapon. Your doubts and fears hold you back, Moho. Why should one as powerful as yourself worry about anything? Aren't you supposed to be a king?"

Moho's face reddened as he scorched Henry with his glare. "I do not fear them, but you should fear me if you do not handle this situation."

I shuddered as memories flooded my mind of the trouble his monster shark had caused. If we hadn't trapped it and stunned it with electric eels, it would still be terrorizing Moku-ola. Now Sid and his eel friends kept it in a coma-like state, waiting for us to figure out how to send it home, wherever home might be. I'd grown a soft spot for the shark I now referred to as Donnie. Part of me hoped we could figure out a way to send him safely home, and the other kinda wanted to get to know him better.

Moho rose and paced around Henry's hammock. "I can't stay above the surface much longer. My sharks need me." He turned his glare on Henry. "Give the flute to me. Show me how to use it."

Henry's mouth twisted into an evil grin. "The flute will not work for you. It will only work for me and my bloodline."

Moho clenched his fists. "No, we share a bloodline. You're lying. It should respond to me as well."

I sucked in my breath. They shared a bloodline? I raised my eyebrow to Akalei, who shook her head. Moho stopped talking and looked in our direction. Could he hear us? We held our breath and slowly stood, tensing our muscles and preparing for a quick escape. He took a few steps in our direction. Just as we spun to make a dash for it, a loud squawk rang out and Maxie dive-bombed Moho's head. Feathers flew as she swiped him across the face with her beak.

I grabbed Akalei's hand and burst into a sprint as Moho screamed in pain and fought off my new hero. We raced neck and neck, putting as much distance as possible between us and Moho.

We made it a good distance before I stopped and gasped for breath, quickly looking back to be sure no one followed us. I bent over and rested my hands on my knees, while gulping some air.

Akalei plopped down. "Now what?" she said, her chest heaving from the exertion.

"Now we…Awwwww!" I screamed and grabbed my pulsating head, collapsing to the ground. A chorus of panicked voices filled my brain like a million hammers pounding against my temples. Pain exploded, blinding me to the world around me. My body curled into a crumpled ball on the sand. My breath quickened as the desperation of thousands sought to overpower my own

20

emotions, choking me with their fear. My mind clung to the here and now, fighting for control amongst the chaos of so many raking through my skull.

Akalei grabbed onto me, worry choking her voice. "Tessa, what is it? What's wrong?"

Sheer willpower pushed through the colliding voices as I forced myself to focus on her question, but struggled to form words with a mouth gone numb. "Something's happened… out… at sea. I think it's an earthquake. Fish and dolphins are diving deep. They're scared." My eyes met hers as I sorted through the cries for clarity. Her gaze grounded me, and reassured me. Suddenly, I understood. "Tsunami."

She froze, then recovered and tugged on my hand. Her eyes wide with panic, and her voice cracking. "Tessa, hurry! We don't have much time. We have to go now!"

I looked at her, grasping the danger. Fear bubbled as my heart kicked into gear. "Rachel. I have to warn Rachel."

CHAPTER 3

PU'UHONUA

REFUGE

We hit the beach at a breakneck pace, kicking sand behind us, determined to beat the wave pummeling toward Lanai. Sweat dampened my skin as I pushed myself harder, faster. The pounding in my skull ebbed to a dull throb, as panic clutched my chest. Akalei matched my stride, her breath quickening next to me. How long before it hit? Would we make it to Rachel in time?

Before reaching the surf, Kupua swam in and waved us down. Slightly out of breath and shaking water from his hair, he shot me a worried look. "Tessa, we have to get back to Moku-ola, now."

I balked, choking on fear for Rachel's safety. "I'm not leaving my sister without a warning. It's not gonna happen."

Kupua grunted. "I've already sent Lizzy to Lanai to warn everyone. Rachel's with my mom and they're all safe. It's handled, Tessa. Your sister will not be in danger but you will be if we waste precious minutes debating the issue. We don't have much time, let's go." He snatched my hand and plunged us into the surf, morphing into a dolphin.

Cool water shocked my overheated muscles and they spasmed in response, pain spiking down my legs. Akalei latched onto my arm with one hand and Kupua's dorsal fin with the other as he sped off, plowing through water in a beeline home. Though the voices had quieted a bit, my mind still spun from the turmoil. Rolling through the ocean, fish and mammals alike, rushed to swim as deep as possible, hoping to avoid getting caught in the powerful wave surging our direction. Some fled towards Moku-ola, seeking sanctuary, and my stomach churned with worry for their safety. Rachel might be safe, but too many others still remained at risk. What had triggered this massive wave?

Moku-ola buzzed with activity. The seriousness of the situation sunk in as I inspected the makeshift refugee camp constructed in the center of our city. Fin and his pod crammed into the ceremonial pool, splashing and squealing, water spouting as they surfaced. Sea lions and Hawaiian monk seals barked and yipped as they jostled for space in every corner. I couldn't hear myself think over the racket. The stench of fish, mingled with sweat and fear, overpowered the usual fresh ocean scent of my home.

Residents of the city mingled among the crushing mob of seals, ensuring all were fed and comfortable and caring for their needs. My heart swelled with gratitude at the selfless nature of my people, many of whom invited ocean guests into their homes, through small pools, making room for all who sought sanctuary in our city. Each home in Moku-ola was uniquely carved and built from surrounding volcanic rock, located over pools feeding into the sea. Secure and safe, Moku-ola provided the perfect refuge.

I plowed through the crowd, checking on my friends, taking stock of who had made it to our safe zone. Lizzy bumped my leg, yelping with worry about her mother, Mimi, who hadn't been seen in hours. She wasn't alone, cries for loved ones consumed me, pounding against my brain, and crushing my soul. Bending over, I covered my head with my arms, seeking to send out calm reassurances, but feeling lost in the chaos of hysteria.

Kupua silently eased behind me and grasped my hand, providing warmth and comfort. I pivoted toward him and his arm wrapped around me, soothing tattered nerves. Noise faded away as I lost myself in the safety of his embrace. After a few minutes, I pulled back and looked into his eyes. "How long before it hits?"

He spoke softly, stroking my hair. "It's hard to know exactly how long before the wave reaches us, but it should be soon. Tessa, you need to come deeper below the city with me. When water pulls from the shore, cries of the stranded will rise, and without protection you'll be driven mad."

I shuddered. My brain already felt like exploding. The constant hammering was wearing down my stamina.

"Is there anything we can do? Anything to prevent such loss?"

He ducked his head, locks of damp hair falling to conceal his expression. Tears pressed against the back of my eyes, grief stinging my heart. I pressed my fingers against my eyelids and worked to gain composure, swallowing the lump pressing against my throat.

Kupua caressed my neck and shoulder. "Ipo, when the waters calm, there will be survivors waiting to be rescued, waiting for you. But now, we must get you safe."

My gaze met his and resolve took hold. My people depended on my strength and endurance; I would not let them down.

He led me to the far end of the city, passing homes where families rushed to secure their passages to the ocean, swiftly cutting off any possibility of flooding water overtaking us. Mother of pearl and brightly colored shells adorned doorways in designs holding specific meaning to the families living within. Polished abalone shimmered, cool and smooth underneath my bare feet.

Finally we reached the edge of the city and discovered a small hole in the volcanic rock just wide enough for one of us to fit through. A rope ladder anchored in the rock draped over the side. Kupua motioned toward the hole. "You first."

My hands went to my hips. "Down there? Really? Will we both fit?"

"It's bigger than it looks. Trust me."

Grabbing hold of the ladder, I lowered myself into the hole, sliding between cool polished rock walls. One step at a time, I descended into a quiet cocoon of warmth. The deeper I went, the more relief came, as pressure against my skull dulled to a distant echo before ceasing altogether. Kupua's weight shook the ladder,

25

causing it to sway as his feet moved from rung to rung above my head. A light glowed beneath us, illuminating our descent with muted shadows. After the final rung my foot cradled into soft sand, and I spun to view a cavern lit by white light emanating through volcanic walls. Peace washed away anxiety as I inhaled the sweet musty fragrance so familiar to me now, with a hint of cinnamon wafting in the air. Silence embraced me like a long lost friend and I relished its return.

Kupua eased down onto the sand, stretching out his legs and tugging me with him.

Closing my eyes, I leaned my head against his chest while he massaged my temples and whispered softly in my ear. "This is the only place in Moku-ola you can escape the calls from our friends of the sea. The walls down here serve as a barrier. You will hear nothing but your own thoughts."

Tension drained through my pores as my muscles relaxed under his fingers, my arms and legs becoming limp.

"I feel so helpless."

"You're never helpless, Tessa. This place exists so you and I can escape voices of the sea and also seek the Creator's voice more clearly."

His words sunk into my soul. How easily I'd forgotten who really held the power to save. Questions whirled though my thoughts. What was I to do? How could I help and protect so many from a tsunami? How could I reach Moho? Why was he poisoning all the fish and how could I stop him? Emotions churned my

26

stomach, threatening to erupt.

The scent of cinnamon intensified until a presence joined us in the cavern. A flash of bright, white light burst out, illuminating every shadowed corner. A voice spoke as a gentle caress. *Give me your worry, Tessa. You cannot stop evil, you can only love.*

Love? I loved, but wasn't more expected? Warmth wrapped me like a blanket, chasing away the chill of uncertainty that seeped into my bones.

Tessa, you are not alone, depend on me. It is I who will work all things out for good. Do you trust me?

"I do trust you," my voice cracked as I answered out loud. "I'm sorry." Truth burned like a fire in my lungs. I allowed the weight of the world to rest on my shoulders. But truth reminded me my Creator carried the weight, not me. I exhaled, releasing my burden like a hand repels a hot coal. My body shook, my lips trembled and tears streamed down my face.

Kupua's finger stroked my cheek. "Feels good to let someone else carry the burden and to know you are never alone, doesn't it?"

"Yeah. I can't believe I forgot who's really in control. Feels good not to have to save the world after all." I curled against Kupua's strong chest and drifted off to sleep, secure and safe.

When I awoke, a sense of renewal coursed through my veins, ready to face whatever waited for us above. I twisted to face Kupua.

"Do you think we've waited long enough? Can we go above?"

He paused. "No, Kele will let us know when it's safe to

return. Someone will come get us. Tessa, I want to know more about your family. Tell me about your sister and how she met Mike."

I sighed. "They met in college. The way Mike tells it, he spotted her in the cafeteria and followed her around like a lost puppy. Of course, Rachel wouldn't go out with him at first, said she didn't have time for dating. So, he asked me out instead."

Kupua stiffened. "What?"

I patted his arm, laughing. "It's not what you think. Mike figured out Rachel didn't want to leave me alone, so she never dated. When he saw us together one day, he marched right up and asked me if I'd like to go to a movie. Being an obnoxious little sister, I said yes, which only irritated Rachel who grudgingly agreed to come along. But, it didn't take Mike long to win her over, not when she saw how kind he was to me."

"Almost makes me feel bad for knocking the guy out...almost."

I giggled at the memory. Kupua had knocked Mike out the first time he'd brought him to Moku-ola, but only so he wouldn't freak out about being transported under water.

"I love the way they look out for each other, always wanting the best for one another. They never made me feel like I was intruding when I lived with them, and believe me, I didn't make it easy."

A voice shouted down to us. "Tessa? Kupua? We need you, now."

Shifting gears, I sprang to my feet. "Coming."

Kupua and I rushed up the ladder where Akalei waited. Dark circles shrouded her eyes, and stains of blood and grime dotted her purple dress. "Hey you two, we have some issues."

Kupua looked around. "Where's Kele?"

"He's dealing with some wounded seals that arrived late. No casualties among our people though. Most got in safe."

I let out a sigh of relief, appreciating any good news. "What are the issues?"

Akalei inhaled. "Okay, first, Kele analyzed the dead fish, and they're full of large amounts of poison; the same poison that paralyzed you and Kupua in Moho's secret cave."

"I knew it!"

Akalei shot me her evil eye and clucked her tongue.

"Sorry…didn't mean to interrupt."

She nodded.

"Next, Eka's family reports she's disappeared. She helped her cousins secure the hatch on their passage to the sea, but afterwards, she vanished. Her mom is requesting a search party form to do a sweep of the surrounding area. Also, Mimi is still missing and Lizzy is sick with worry, we have fish and shrimp stranded and in need of rescue…oh, and this is really weird, no sharks have been spotted anywhere, they're just…gone." She exhaled, her shoulders deflating with weariness.

I leaned into her. "Thank you for taking care of everything, but now it's time for you to rest." She gave me a weak smile.

Kupua placed his hand on my shoulder, his eyebrow raised in

question. I smiled back at him, organizing our to-do list in my head. "I'll rescue the fish and shrimp, you assemble a team to find Mimi and Eka. We'll figure out what to do about the poison later and the sharks will have to wait."

"Good plan."

I turned back to my tired friend. "Akalei, you and Kele handle things here, I'll take Lizzy with me. And…get some rest…that's an order."

She gave me a quick hug and took off to find Kele. I watched her go, respect and affection bursting from my chest. I knew how lucky I was to have a friend like her. I glanced back at Kupua.

"If fish are dying from the same poison used to protect the flute, it confirms our fears that Henry and Moho are behind all of this." Right after I'd been crowned queen, we discovered Henry's flute. It had been protected by poison water, which paralyzed us for days and almost killed us both.

He tapped his head with his finger, smiling. "Adding *finding the flute* to my to-do list right now." He tugged me into a hug, his breath warm against my ear. "Be careful, Ipo."

I stood on my tiptoes and kissed his cheek. "Always am." He raised his eyebrow at me again, but I spun and jogged off to find Lizzy before he could change his mind about our separate assignments.

CHAPTER 4

NALOWALE

MISSING

Lizzy and I snuggled into soft sand, my legs heavy as cement bricks, exhausted from throwing fish and shrimp into the sea. We didn't save them all, but we saved most of them. Aching muscles cramped in both arms, burning from overuse which is why I'd chosen not to head home without some rest. Lizzy nuzzled my stomach and I slid my hand over her silky fur, stroking her neck as she groaned in pleasure. Fish and salt mingled in the air leaving a tangy aftertaste in my mouth. Sunset faded behind the horizon, and darkness crept onto the beach as we lay gazing at the stars. Moonlight shimmered across the ocean while siren calls from humpback whales echoed off the water. My mind drifted, fraying at the edges. Weariness crept over me and my eyelids grew heavy.

Next thing I knew, sunshine warmed my face and Lizzy's flipper bounced across my arm. Prickles tingled my hand as I shifted positions and withdrew it from under Lizzy's weight. Scooting upright, I scanned the beach for any sign of life. Seagulls swooped low, searching for breakfast and in the distance a group of children danced in the surf, their giggles drifting over the breeze.

I nudged Lizzy and she growled, flipping in an attempt to ignore me. I couldn't believe we'd slept all night on the beach. Kupua must be going crazy with worry.

Sid called out from beneath the waves, reporting no sign of any sharks and worried Kupua hadn't returned from his search. Unease tickled my senses, but I shoved it aside. Kupua could easily be delayed if following a lead. After all, I hadn't returned yet either.

I heaved to my feet and tapped my toes on Lizzy's back, sprinkling bits of sand in her fur. "Time to head back and see what's happening in Moku-ola, sleepy head." She shook herself and grudgingly plodded after me into the water, growling and moaning her complaints.

Back in the city, things had calmed. All the sea lions had departed, leaving piles of stale fish bones in their wake. An eerie quiet replaced the chaos of yesterday. Teens armed with baskets wandered the paths, cleaning up debris and sharing stories of the tsunami in hushed tones. Most people resumed their normal routines or returned home to survey damage; all but Kele. He paced back and forth across the large open room overlooking the city, his bare feet squeaking across the floor. "Kele, take a break, you're wearing out the floor."

"Eh Tessa, my brah no back, dis no good. Let's hele on out,

you gef 'em, ah?"

"Kele, it hasn't been that long, he's probably still searching for Mimi and Eka. You know he wouldn't give up until he found them." Lizzy bumped my hand and yipped, projecting worry for her mother.

Akalei stood, wringing her hands. "I don't know Tessa, something isn't right, it isn't like Kupua not to return home or at least send word about being delayed. Maybe Kele's right, maybe we should check on him."

Kele nodded at Akalei. "Ya, we go an finz our bruddah."

The unease I'd felt earlier returned, driving me to pace the floor alongside Kele, hands on my hips. "Okay, let's think. Where might he have been searching?"

Silence.

"What? No sense waiting here. Let's see if we can find out what's going on!"

Kele yanked me into a hug, smiling, relief shining in his eyes.

"Tanks teeta."

Akalei joined him and I found myself being squeezed until I gasped for breath. Akalei leaned backwards and chimed, "Sorry, it's just we didn't expect you to agree with us so fast, kinda surprised us."

I rolled my eyes. "That's not fair, I agree all the time!"

She patted my shoulder. "Sure you do."

"Hey, hanging around here won't help us get answers and

when it comes to Kupua I don't want to take chances. I know he can take care of himself but if Moho's involved he may need our help."

We started with wide sweeps around the city, working our way farther and farther out to sea. A few miles out we ran into Elmo and his mom. They hadn't seen Kupua. They also hadn't seen any sharks. My heart skipped, this wasn't good. Where were all the sharks and why hadn't anyone seen Kupua? Where would he have gone to search?

I ordered Lizzy out in a different direction to check for any sign of him. Surely someone had seen something, he couldn't have disappeared without anyone noticing…right?

Akalei bumped my arm and I jerked, wound up in my own thoughts. She pointed down. We floated at the edge of the chasm, where Moho had released the monster shark now imprisoned below. I shuddered. Donnie still slept in a hidden cavern, kept in a coma until we figured out what to do with him. We had to check *everything* out if we were going to find Kupua, so I steeled myself, grasped Akalei's hand, and kicked into the yawning black hole.

Whispers hummed in my head, like bees swarming a hive...eels burrowed deep in the walls of the chasm thrummed with chatter. I paused at the first hole hoping to coax one of the shy creatures out to talk. A young male speckled with yellow spots poked his head out, nervously withdrawing it again quickly, but not before introducing himself as Edgar. Edgar had never talked to a queen before and quivered in his hideaway, fearful to approach. I hovered outside, shooting reassuring thoughts his way. When he reluctantly emerged I stroked his long, flowing, silky body, allowing him to wrap around my arm. Slowly, his confidence built, until he found his voice.

Edgar informed us rumors of fish dying in the deep waters off the island of Catalina near California spread among his friends. Some eels spoke of a large number of great white sharks gathered there, as if being summoned. Word traveled fast in the ocean and secrets were almost impossible to keep. I gave Edgar a kiss and thanked him for his help as he uncoiled and slid into his hole.

As we descended farther into the chasm, we heard similar stories. Dying fish and a large gathering of sharks did not bode well for any peaceful sea creature. This had Moho written all over it. I could only hope Kupua wasn't in the middle of whatever was happening in the waters off Catalina.

Once we reached the bottom, we shimmied through a hidden passage to the pool holding Donnie. Air locked tunnels existed in many parts of the ocean, but especially near volcanos where caves were plentiful. Megalodons didn't belong in our time, and Donnie's very presence baffled us, leaving us at a total loss as to what to do with him.

Akalei, and I entered the small cavern where energy-charged waves rippled through the pool as electric eels zapped Donnie into a coma-like state. His brain slept, no pain, no worry. His dorsal fin bobbed above the surface as he gently rocked with the rippling water, like a baby in a cradle, looking almost innocent...almost. Static pricked along my arms like a thousand tiny needles, electrifying the air and causing our hair to stand on end.

I sighed. "No sign of Kupua. Nothing going on here, let's get back to Kele and keep looking."

Akalei squeezed my hand. "We'll find him, Tessa."

"I know. I just hope it's in time." I motioned toward Donnie. "I wish I knew what to do with Donnie. We can't release him but I don't like holding him captive, it can't be good for his health."

"You saved a lot of lives by capturing him, Tessa. You had no choice."

"Maybe." I retreated into the tunnel, glancing one last time over my shoulder at Donnie, a wisp of regret tugging my heart.

At the top of the chasm Lizzy and Sid waited for us with more information.

Lizzy twirled in circles around me, darting close, then shooting away, anxiety rolling off her fur. Mimi and Eka had been seen together, leaving the city at about the same time. Lizzy whirled, wound like a spinning top, frantic to find her mother. I reached out and rubbed my hand across her head as she whooshed past me. Kele chased after her but she quickly outdistanced him before angling back in our direction. Kele shook his fist at her, his face red and flustered. I waved at him.

"I know of a cave nearby where we can rest and discuss what to do next. Follow me." Kele swam within an arm's distance from me, tension vibrating off him like a current, setting my own nerves on edge.

Once we settled in the cave I rounded on him. "Kele, what is up with you? You are always the calm one…I need you to be the calm one."

"Tessa, garans dis all bout no good for nothing baga, Moho. I nervous fo my brah, Kupua. Dis story bout da sharks is all crazy. I all buckaloose, wanna fight." He started pacing the beach, shaking his arms out in front of him.

Heat climbed my back until I couldn't take it anymore. Throwing my arms in the air I raised my voice. "You think *I'm* not worried? I don't have the luxury to fall apart. Kupua is depending on me, on all of us. If anything happens to him, it's on *me*; I sent him out on the search. I don't even want to think about it. Snap out of it, Kele. We have work to do!"

Akalei stepped in front of him and he immediately halted, his head and shoulders drooping. She wrapped her arms around his neck and snuggled him close. He let out a sigh and his whole body relaxed against hers. She swiveled her head to catch my attention, tears welling in her eyes, then stretched out her hand to me. I clasped it, already choking on regret at raising my voice. She tugged me into a group hug and we stood there for several minutes just taking comfort from one another, acknowledging our silent apologies. Without speaking we released our grip and plopped onto the sand.

Akalei broke the silence. "If sharks are gathering in Catalina, and fish are dying, we have no choice but to go there and investigate. Kupua must have heard the same rumors. I bet we find him there."

I nodded in agreement. "Moho is likely behind the deaths. He probably has something to do with Kupua, Eka and Mimi all being missing. I'm sure it's not a coincidence. Since we know he doesn't have the flute, my guess is Henry's involved somehow as well. The big question is why? What do they gain from killing off fish?"

Akalei shrugged. "Wish I knew. Seems random to me."

"Maybe da buggas don't mean to kill da fish, maybe dey doin sometin else and it jus' happens. Brutal, but an akkcident."

I frowned at him. "Maybe. But it just doesn't make sense. Do you think the Lua Pele's connected to any of this? Moho's been in its lair and seems to have some connection with it." I shuddered, remembering the stench when I'd pulled Eka from its hole. I never wanted to find out firsthand what caused such a putrid smell.

Akalei dropped her head in her hands. "Does it really matter? I say we pay Catalina a visit and figure the rest out later. Sitting around is making me nervous."

Kele added, "Befo we go, I need get mo medicine fo da poision, jus in case."

"Okay, we have a plan," I announced. "Kele, go back and get whatever supplies you need. We'll rest here, but hurry, okay? Catalina's not exactly close."

Kele plunged into the water while Akalei and I nestled into the sand. Kupua's absence bore a hole in my heart. Thinking he might be in danger twisted my stomach into knots. Danger seemed to nip at our heels wherever we went.

CHAPTER 5

HU'IHU'I KAI

CHILLY SEA

Icy water chilled deep into my bones, cramping and aching fatigued muscles. We'd started early, the moment Kele returned with his supplies. Long past time to stop and rest, I swam towards the bottom and the others followed. Visibility worsened until Kele and Akalei transformed into murky green shadows, evoking a longing for the clear Hawaiian waters we'd left.

Our travel attracted the attention of a school of barracuda who felt we needed some "protection" and surrounded us as we swam, intimidating curious fish attempting to get a closer look at our group. Their jaws jutted forward in a fierce expression matched only by their aggressive posture as they ambushed unsuspecting fish who happened to swim too close.

Sid replaced Lizzy as my ambassador in route and didn't trust the barracuda, mostly because they crowded him, posturing and nipping at floating tentacles. Every once in a while he would defiantly squirt ink in their eyes, forcing them to give him space.

We groped around rock formations along the sea floor, searching for an open-air hideaway to spend the night and get some much needed rest. Dense kelp obstructed our ability to see farther than the few feet our wrist-bands illuminated. Kele discovered a promising tunnel which we quickly found led to an underground grotto deep within a system of caves.

Low ceilings sloped to the ground creating a shallow cavern with just enough room to stand. Bits of broken shells formed a coarse beach with a gentle dip sloping into the water. Puffs of mist formed before my mouth as my breath collided with air not much warmer than the sea. Lichen-covered rocks glowed under the green light of our wrist-bands like glow in the dark stickers my sister used to put on her wall.

Barracuda posted themselves outside the entrance as sentries, stubbornly insisting on keeping watch. Sid scrunched himself into a crevice, clouding the water with ink and mumbling something about bullies. I felt a little like a celebrity with my own posse.

We all collapsed on the beach, muscles weary from our long swim. Sticky sea water dripped from my hair, stinging my eyes and goose bumps shivered up my arms. I missed Kupua. His presence brought me strength, and I needed some of that right now.

Akalei plopped beside me, her teeth chattering as she rubbed her hands up and down her arms, chasing away her own goose bumps. "Wwwwow…it's ccccold here."

Kele sat next to her, stroking her back in a gallant attempt to generate heat. "Post to wear wet suit in dis moana," he announced, like we hadn't noticed.

"Now you tell us," I snapped, immediately regretting my words.

He gave me the stink eye. "You da luna (boss), do somtin bout it."

"You're right. I can do something about this." I summoned my fastest friends, the dolphin and asked them to retrieve some wet suits from Moku-ola. Fin responded right away. I grinned at Kele and raised my chin.

"Okay, I took care of it. By the time we wake up, our wetsuits should be delivered."

Kele pulled a strange-looking square rock out of his backpack and placed it on the sand in front of us. Blacker than coal, it slowly glowed brighter and brighter as heat and red light emanated from its dark center. Akalei wiggled closer. I waved my hands over the rock soaking up its warmth. "Pretty sick, where did you get it?"

He smiled. "Dis rock mo bettah dan any rock. Find only in secret spot me an my brah, Kupua know bout."

I narrowed my eyes at him. "Kele, our man of mystery, you never cease to surprise me." Our small fire rock heated the tight quarters until our goose bumps vanished and we relaxed all toasty and dry.

Kele plucked dried seaweed wrapped around rice patties out of his backpack and we ravenously inhaled it. Swimming worked up an appetite. I eased back onto gravelly sand as the last bite slid down my throat, satisfying my growling stomach.

"What do you think about sending barracuda ahead to scout for us? Moho won't suspect them since they live in these waters and they might discover information we'd miss, not knowing the area the way they do."

Akalei smiled. "I like the idea. Better we know what we're swimming into."

Kele didn't look so sure, his nose wrinkling into a frown. "I dunnah like da idea, da poison, ass why. Dey maybe get hurt."

I bit my lip. "I forgot about the poison, but I doubt they're using it. If all the sharks are in the area, Moho wouldn't risk their lives. We have a better chance knowing what we're walking into if the barracuda scout for us. If we make a mistake, Kupua could die, if he's even there."

He dropped his head, thinking, then nodded. "Kay den."

I nudged his shoulder and his thick torso didn't even budge. "I'll tell them to be careful, to abort the plan at the first sign of danger."

He rubbed his head, his short cropped hair popping back into place as his fingers ran through it.

With nothing more to say, we all dug out our spots in the sand and drifted off to sleep. My thoughts called out to Kupua, hoping he might be close enough to hear me, but only silence answered. He would answer if he could and that worried me. This was the longest we'd been separated since we'd met, and I didn't like it one bit. Surviving the death of my parents had been hard, but the thought of losing Kupua brought on panic beyond anything I'd experienced. I pushed those thoughts away into a locked chamber in my heart, hoping I'd never have to open that door.

A shiver woke me. I lurched upright and glanced over at Kele and Akalei who both slept soundly just a few feet away, the gentle rise and fall of their chests in perfect sync. I listened. Distress calls filtered from the surface. Somebody cried out for help, tugging on my heart for a response. I rose, brushing coarse sand off my legs and eased into the water, not wanting to wake my friends but being pulled toward the call like a magnet. On the way out of the tunnel, Sid coiled a tentacle around my wrist, suction cups clamping onto skin in an attempt to stop me. I peeled him off, freeing my arm. "I have to go. I'm the queen, it's my responsibility."

He trailed behind me, grumbling with a tentacle fastened around my ankle. Stubborn octopus. Urgency quickened my pace as I swam to the surface. Early morning light pushed out the night's darkness, shooting shafts of light into the dreary water.

Panicked cries for assistance intensified as I drew closer to the surface. Two dolphins trapped in nets cast by a tuna boat struggled against the cords holding them captive. Writhing, tangled, and desperate for air, they didn't have much time left. I yanked my knife from the strap around my leg and kicked toward them, commanding Sid to back off. He reluctantly released my leg, tentacles curling back around his body. The tricky part was going to be avoiding the notice of any surface dwellers awake on the boat. I

43

sent waves of reassurance ahead of me, hoping to calm the dolphins' frantic minds.

Blood trailed through the water, leaving a scent of metal and fear lingering in its wake. Not good. The remaining dolphin pod circled the net, visibly upset, darting in and nipping at the lines attempting to pull their family free. No sign of any humans above water, for now. At least something worked in my favor.

The trapped dolphins were young teenagers, Rip and Bailey. They thrashed and squealed, lurching the massive catch of tuna back and forth. Swimming underneath, I instructed them to be still. My hands shook as I sawed through netting, frantic to create a hole big enough for them both to escape. My fingers burned and reddened as I hacked away at thick nylon fibers, painfully aware of Rip and Bailey's urgent need to breathe like a weight on my chest. With several more slashes the opening widened.

Rip slipped free first, sliding past me and leaping out of the water for air. Swarms of tuna poured from the net after him, giving me slack in the lines to work with. Blood trickled from Baily's fin as netting cut deeper into her flesh. She struggled to free herself but every move only tangled her further. Stretching cords away from her skin, I sliced carefully until she slowly squirmed free. A sigh of relief escaped me as she surfaced and took a breath, rubbing against her brother. Remaining tuna dumped into the sea around me, ecstatic with newfound freedom. I spared a moment of disgust for the surface dwellers' methods and lack of concern. Human indifference posed the greatest danger to my ocean friends.

Dark thoughts exploded into my awareness as dolphins circled around me. Rip and Bailey joined me in the center, surrounded by their family. Sharks approached, attracted by blood in the water and seeking prey. Being spotted by sharks was not on my agenda for the day. I grabbed hold of Rip and Bailey's dorsal fin and they plunged me toward the bottom, speeding away from danger. Their pod stayed at a distance to provide a decoy for the sharks, pledging their loyalty and commitment to protect their queen.

Before we reached the cave entrance, barracuda intercepted and surrounded us, providing further camouflage. Jamming together, barracuda glided next to me, shoulder to shoulder pushing and jockeying for position. Sid swam among them, his tentacles whipping out and snatching at my legs. Once locked on, he used his free tentacles to push away barracuda pressing too close. He has issues.

Kele and Akalei were up and prepared to leave, our wetsuits already delivered by Fin and his pod. My nerves hummed from the thrill of the rescue as I shook water from my hair. Sid parked himself at the water's edge, blurting out some not so happy thoughts about putting my life at risk.

Kele marched over and shook his finger in my face. "Tessa, you lolo, goin out alone. I get all huhu, crazy, wen you do dat, stop it."

I cast a beseeching look in Akalei's direction. She caught Kele's arm and tugged him back a step. "Kele, ease off. Tessa's smart. If she takes a risk, it's for a good reason."

45

"That's right, Kele. You know I have no choice when I hear a call for help, it's who I have been called to be. I'm queen and responsible for all life in this sea. You know that."

He looked down at his feet, face in his hands. "I care 'fo you, dat why I worry…go all crazy."

His words slammed into me like a brick wall. Kele cared about me, looked out for me. He did his best to care for all of us. I took a deep breath. "I'm sorry Kele, I didn't mean to worry you, but I am queen and it's my job to respond to calls for help." I leaned forward and put my arms around him.

He hugged me fiercely then stepped back to wipe his eyes. "Just let me go wit you next time."

I touched his arm. "Kele, I can't promise to always include you, but I am always careful. You have to trust me."

He glanced over at Akalei, a plea for support in his eyes. She rolled her eyes at him and smiled at me. "Tessa's right Kele, she can take care of herself. Trust her."

His head drooped with defeat. "I giv'up, but don't like it."

I swiveled toward Akalei and she handed me a wetsuit. "Here, put this on, it'll help with the chill."

CHAPTER 6

MAHOE

TWINS

Barracuda scouts reported from patrol. Brutus, the leader, informed us of a large gathering of great white sharks just off Catalina, close to Two Harbors, located at the Isthmus on the south side of the island. He discovered secret chambers in the deeper water nearby, places capable of hiding Moho, where surface dwellers would never dare venture. Dead Garibaldi fish were sighted near Avalon and had the local community of bat rays and flying fish in a frenzy, abandoning familiar waters for safety.

I shouted orders as I tugged on the wetsuit, shoving my legs through resistant rubber and wiggling it into place. "Looks like Two Harbors is the place to be. We should split up. Kele you approach from the South with Brutus and friends. Akalei, Sid and I will come from the North. Smaller groups will attract less attention. No one is to go near Avalon until we have a better handle on what's happening." They all nodded.

After zipping my suit I slid into the water with a sigh, no more shivering. I missed the warmth of Hawaiian waters, but at least the wetsuit provided some protection against the chill. Rip, Bailey and their pod offered to convey us the rest of the way, so we each latched onto a fin and sped off.

A few miles off the coast of Catalina we split up and said good-bye to our dolphin friends. Kelp forest surrounded the island and loomed over us, providing great cover. Towering stalks of green swayed with the currents, their blades brushing against me as I passed through. Now and then, a rubbery leaf tangled around my wrist, causing me to shake my hand until it drifted off, leaving a slimy residue. Bat rays glided past us, disappearing among the stalks after sharing a warning about dying fish. Fear tumbled through the ocean currents like a virus spreading on contact to everything it touched. Hoards of fish sought safety by fleeing to deeper waters.

Akalei and I weaved in and out of kelp searching for the entrance to the secret chamber Brutus had found. Massive green stalks stretched toward the surface like the giant redwood trees in Sequoia I'd seen as a child. Still no sign of any sharks. Hopefully they weren't all down south in Kele's path.

Sid crept along the sandy bottom, tentacles squeezing into every crevice and curling around rocks as he explored. Silt puffed up from the sea floor making it difficult to see. He located an entrance buried under a rock formation, hidden among thick seaweed. Smooth boulders littered the ocean floor. Akalei pushed forward to enter but

I grabbed her arm. It was my job to go in first.

With just enough room to squeeze my head and shoulders through, arms scraping on the rocks, I squirmed into the tunnel. A blast of warm water caressed my cheeks and I sighed with pleasure. With my arms in front of me, I hauled myself forward until the tunnel opened enough to swim. Akalei caught up to me and clasped my hand. Sid stayed behind, keeping guard over our escape route.

Using our wristbands to navigate the dark tunnel, green tinted light bounced off walls and sent small fish scurrying for cover into the cracks and crevices among rocks. The tunnel went on forever and I experienced a moment of claustrophobic panic, calmed only by Akalei's presence next to me. As we approached a fork in our path we paused, not sure which direction to choose. A soft pinging emanated to the right of where we floated so we swam in that direction. As the sound grew louder, the tunnel took a turn and we broke the surface, finding ourselves in an underwater cave, at last.

Water lapped against rocks, echoing off walls barely visible in the chilly darkness. We eased onto a gravel beach, trying not to make any sound and hoping to avoid detection in case Henry or Moho lurked nearby. My breath misted in front of me like puffs of fog on an early morning. Our bands provided enough light to illuminate our next steps as we followed the pinging. Several offshoots to the main cave veered off both left and right. I bit my lip and whispered, "I can't tell which way the sound is coming from, can you?"

Akalei frowned and shook her head, her teeth chattering.

"No. But look down there." She pointed into the opening on our right. "Can you see it?"

I squinted, straining to see what she saw. "Maybe. It's not quite as dark that way. There's a flicker of light."

She smiled. "Right. I vote we check it out."

"Sounds good to me."

Gravel crunched under our feet, causing me to cringe with every step, worried our presence might be noticed by the wrong people. The farther we crept, the brighter the light grew until we could see the tunnel clearly, including the solid stone barrier blocking the path.

Torches hung from the walls, casting shadows against the rock wall, which danced as flames flickered. Pieces of dried driftwood fueled the fires, set inside rusty tin cans latched to the wall by iron-latticed scoops on hooks. Someone had definitely been down here, recently.

"We must be in the right place, these torches are here for a reason and I'm guessing Moho's behind it." I examined the walls, running my hands over the smooth cold surface searching for a clue or anything to help us know what to do next.

The pinging silenced, replaced by the pounding of my heart as I desperately inspected every inch of rock, dropping to my knees and digging in gravel with my bare hands. If we couldn't go forward, maybe there was a way down. The place wasn't lit for nothing.

Beneath gravel, my hand hit a metal latch. Akalei kneeled next to me and helped shovel gravel aside until a large trap door imbedded in the floor lay exposed. She looked at me, silent questioning in her eyes.

"Wonder where this leads?" My heart leapt in my throat. Could Kupua be on the other side? My stomach lurched with hope.

I pressed my ear to the floor, trying to hear anything that would give us a clue as to what lay below. Cold metal bit into my skin, but I couldn't detect any hint of sound or movement. I gripped the latch with shaking hands and tugged. Nothing. Akalei added her strength to the effort and together we heaved, falling backwards when it didn't budge. After several attempts, metal creaked and groaned, billowing dust into the air and overwhelming my nostrils with the scent of must and earth. We swung the door until it crashed onto gravel, all hopes of being sneaky lost as the sound echoed our arrival. I waved my hands to disperse the dust and sneezed as it tickled my nose. Sticking my arm into the black expanse so my wristband might reveal what lay beneath, I held my breath. A man stepped out from the shadows below. Kupua.

A gasp escaped my lips and joy exploded in my heart, until I saw his leg chained to the wall. A manacle circling his ankle had rubbed him raw and dried blood covered his foot. He wore nothing but ripped swim trunks and mud caked his arms and legs. He lifted a finger to his mouth, motioning us to keep silent. I swung my legs into the opening and dropped next to him, throwing my arms around his neck. He reeked of dirt and sweat, but I didn't care, I'd found him.

He squeezed me tight but quickly pulled back, frowning.

"You should not have come here, it's too dangerous. Where's Kele, didn't he come with you? I'll strangle him if he let you come alone."

I raised an eyebrow at him. "Too dangerous? Hey, I'm the queen, remember, danger is what I do now."

He nudged me against the wall, whispering. "Moho's here, and so is Henry. You can't stay, Tessa. We can't risk you being captured."

I jerked my arm back. "I'm not leaving you here. We are both getting out of this place as soon as we get these chains off you. How did you get here anyway?"

"Someone knocked me out while I was searching for Mimi and I woke in this cell, chained. Since I can't change shape without water I'm stuck. Moho's been here once and he said nothing about why he took me but I can guess it's to lure you here." Frustration rolled off him, his muscles tensing, fists clenching, the veins in his neck bulging. He paced back and forth limping slightly, his shackles clinking against the floor.

Cell walls surrounded us, not more than a few feet across, leaving room for little else besides a bucket of water in the corner. An iron door with a small viewing hole had been built into the rock. I attempted to yank it open but it held tight, locked and solid. The place stank of mold and decay, tinged with urine. Kupua's chains anchored into the ground, securely fastened and welded together. I knelt to examine his ankle and choked on anger at how he'd been treated. His skin was raw and bleeding under the manacle, but not yet infected, thank goodness.

52

Akalei poked her head down the opening. "Hey you two, what's the plan? We can't hang around here all day."

I kicked the iron door. "There's no plan. We never have a plan. Kupua's chained, but I'm not leaving until we get him free. We're all getting out of this place together."

He grunted behind me.

"I've got an idea…" Her head suddenly jerked back and disappeared. Grunts and shrieks above sucked the air from my lungs and I seized hold of rock and started climbing, heart in my throat. Before reaching the top, Henry's face filled the opening, sneering at me.

"So nice to see you again, Tessa. Lose something?" He heaved Akalei into the air and tossed her in the cell. She landed on her side with a thud, groaning in pain. Releasing my grip on the wall I fell next to her, inspecting her arms and legs for broken bones.

"Are you hurt?"

She moaned, rubbing her head. "No, just feeling really stupid."

Henry laughed.

The door next to Kupua burst open and another Henry stepped in. He gawked at his counterpart. "Been having fun again, bro?"

Kupua clutched my hand, as we said in unison, "Twins."

Moho charged through the door, shoving Henry number two aside like an unwanted toy. Tension electrified the air as everyone froze. Moho's dark eyes filled with contempt as he swept his gaze across the scene. "A family reunion, how nice."

CHAPTER 7

'ANO

CHARACTER

Three of us stood, chained, in the center of a dark, musty room we'd been hustled into by the evil twins. Stagnant, moldy air tickled my throat and threatened to bring up my last meal. Water drained through a grate positioned beneath our feet, and trickled somewhere far below, echoing through the shaft with every drop. Chains looped around my legs and wrists, binding me to Akalei and Kupua and all three of us secured by a bolt in the floor. Movement became slow and sluggish under the weight of my bonds, even moving an arm proved painful.

Moho strutted around us, a smirk of satisfaction plastered on his face, his skin covered in a sheen of sweat. Henry and his twin, Sam, stood on either side of the door, both with arms crossed in front of their chests. Sam wore a t-shirt, slightly wrinkled, while Henry looked pressed and starched as usual.

Moho didn't know I could communicate while out of water. It was an advantage I intended to use as I closed my eyes and let Sid know we'd been captured. Sid's response was immediate; help was coming. I opened my eyes and raised my chin. "Moho, why do you continue to fight against your own people? Why won't you come back and live with us in Moku-ola?"

He remained focused on Kupua and stopped nose to nose with his brother, intense challenge flaring in his eyes. "Reconcile to what? To watching you have everything, leaving me with nothing but walking in your shadow? I don't need your pity. I am stronger, I should be king." He held his arms wide. "Tell me brother, if you are the better candidate for king, why are you in chains?"

Kupua lifted his head high and rattled his chains. "You're correct, you are my brother, a brother I will always love. Chains do not define a king. Compassion for others, courage to face your mistakes, those are characteristics needed to be king. You have turned your back on love and your heart shrivels in bitterness. Choose differently my brother."

Moho grasped Kupua's throat and growled. "Don't speak to me of love. You have robbed me of love and now it's time to pay the price."

Seeing Moho's hand strangling Kupua's throat sent me spiraling into panic, yanking at my chains. "Moho, what do you want from us? Why have you chained us?"

He released Kupua and wheeled to face me, sneering. "I'm not taking any chances with you this time. I tried to be nice, but no

56

more."

Nice? When had he been nice? Somehow I'd missed his good guy period. "Okay, but what do you plan to do? Even if you kill us the people of our city will never follow you."

"Let's all take a little walk and find out."

Despite fear clawing inside my stomach I straightened my shoulders and held my head high, refusing to allow fear a place in my heart. Kupua's strength joined mine as we stood side by side, prepared for whatever Moho might have planned. Akalei inched closer, adding her love and support. I stretched my hand toward her and she laced her trembling fingers with mine, Whatever we faced, we faced it together.

Henry and his twin stepped forward, unlocking our chains from the floor and jerking us through the door. As we stumbled down a dark hall, Akalei bumped her body against mine, a silent encouragement. Kupua positioned himself in front, between us and the twins. Sam looked over his shoulder, his expression shifting between fear and confusion. Maybe he wasn't on board with Henry's plan. Perhaps his loyalty wavered.

Akalei whispered as we walked. "I can't believe we're all in chains."

"Yeah, comes with the whole rescue package I ordered. Too bad there's no room service."

"Be serious, Tessa. We have to figure out something fast, before he separates us."

I swallowed down panic. I hadn't considered the possibility

57

we might get separated. Kupua glanced back at me and mouthed, "We'll be fine, don't worry."

I flashed him a weak smile and leaned in to speak into Akalei's ear. "Don't forget, backup is on the way."

"That's what I'm afraid of. Kele won't expect us to be chained and he'll be outnumbered. I don't want his big stubborn head to get hurt."

Sam swung his head, giving us a quick scan before resuming our march down a tunnel. I nudged Akalei. "Shhhhh…it'll be okay."

We halted at the edge of a ledge looking over crystal clear water, crammed with writhing sharks. Brown and grey bodies thrashed against each other, splashing water onto the ledge. My feet slipped on the slick, wet surface, causing me to stumble forward into Kupua's back. He grunted on impact but didn't move, swiveling his head to check on me. "You okay?"

"Besides being chained, I'm fine," I told him, regaining my balance and straightening. "But who knows for how long by the look of that mob." I inclined my head toward the ravenous hoard of sharks waiting for dinner to be tossed their way.

He tilted his head back to get a better look at me. "Tessa, you may not be able to control them but they still won't harm you, not as long as you are the crowned queen."

"What about the rest of you?"

He shifted positions, turning towards Moho, his mouth set in a grim line. My stomach did a couple flips. I guess I had my answer, and I didn't like it one bit and neither did my stomach.

Moho perched on the overhang, dangling his legs over the side and calmly dipped his hand in the water, stilling all activity among his sharks, as if his mood and theirs were in perfect sync. Consuming hunger emanated off the sharks, like a deep, unending void, piercing my soul. Moho's connection to the sharks felt strong, a bond similar to family bonds I'd experienced before, rooted in instinct and survival. Each shark brushed against his hand, rubbing and churning to compete for his touch, lingering under his hand and feet as if reluctant to part from his presence.

Moho glared over his shoulder, eyes black. "Bring Kupua to me."

My heart plummeted as Henry shoved Kupua closer to the edge. I lurched forward, but was jerked back by my chains, held tight by Sam, who unlocked the links connecting Kupua to Akalei and I. Kupua cast a glance at me, warning me to stay put, before he focused on his brother, his back straight, chin lifted.

Moho's dark gaze landed on me. "This choice belongs to you, Tessa. I am giving you a chance to spare Kupua's life. All you have to do is marry me, renounce Kupua's right to the throne and crown me your king. If not, Kupua meets his death with my friends here." He inclined his head toward the sharks and tails thrashed with increased ferocity, whipping water into white foam. A large tiger breeched the surface with death in its black eyes and ragged teeth jutting from its jaw.

My legs trembled, threatening to collapse and I struggled for words that might somehow reach Moho's hardened heart. "Moho, I have offered you love and forgiveness, both of which you have spurned. You ask for marriage, for a crown, but marriage and being king is not about power, it's about loving and caring for more than yourself. If you want to be king, first seek a king's heart – learn to love others."

Moho opened his mouth to speak just as an iron door crashed open and Eka burst into the room. With her tear-streaked face red with anger, hair in disarray and her voice a shrill shriek, she pointed at Moho. "What do you mean she has to marry you? You said you loved *me*, you promised to marry *me*. You said things would be different, that you no longer desired the throne! Why did you lie?"

Moho froze, his piercing eyes focused on me. He flicked his hand at Henry. "Get her out of here."

Henry stalked over and seized Eka around the waist, lifting her like a rag doll. She flung her body forward, screaming, kicking and punching him to no avail. "Let go of me," she wailed as he tossed her over his shoulder and lugged her back through the iron door, grunting a few times as her fists pummeled his back. Her cries struck me to the core like arrows in the heart. Moho was responsible for her father's death, yet she couldn't stay away from him. Anger burned my eyes as I turned my gaze back to Moho.

"Seems like you're already taken, Moho."

His mouth twisted into a smile that never reached his eyes. "I told you once before you will be my queen or no one's. You speak of love for others…well, I'm giving you an opportunity to choose now and show how much you care for Kupua's life. Do you love him enough to save him? It really doesn't matter to me, either way I will be your king."

Before I could respond, Kupua's voice rang out, clear and strong, commanding our attention. "Brother, watch and learn the true lesson of courage, love and trust." Kupua leapt off the ledge, breaking free of his chains and transformed into a great white shark. Chaos broke out as we all surged forward and Moho dove into the water after him.

"Kupua…nooooo," I screamed, my voice echoing through the cavern. But it was too late to stop what he had set into motion.

Kele swung up unexpectedly from under the ledge, snatched our chains and launched Sam into the thrashing water, his keys clanging to the floor. Maybe the sharks would have a meal after all.

Kele scooped the keys and unlocked us. As soon as the chains fell from my wrists and ankles, I rushed for the water but Kele caught me, lurching me backwards. "No, we go dis way. My brah is good, he will meet us in Avalon."

I struggled, fighting against his tight grip on my wrist. "No, he needs our help, I can't leave him."

Akalei moved in front of me, her voice soft but tense with urgency. "Tessa, we must hurry. Think about it, Kupua is most powerful in the water, he can handle this situation. If you jump in, he will be distracted, trying to protect you. Calm yourself and you will know we're right, you can sense for yourself the truth of our words."

I stilled, my body limp in Kele's arms. My mind reached for Kupua's. They were right, he felt confident he could handle the situation and was broadcasting loudly for us to escape quickly. Relief eased the tension pricking at my muscles. I nodded to Kele. "You're right. Release me and let's get out of here."

We re-traced our path back to the cell we'd found Kupua in earlier and climbed the rocky wall out of Moho's hideaway. My heart rebelled at moving in the opposite direction of Kupua, but I forced my steps forward, like pressing against an invisible force field. Kele quickened the pace and had us jogging toward the water, motioning with his hand for us to hurry. "Hoh, get movin, we gotta get outta here!"

We skidded to a stop at the gravel beach and found both Lizzy and Sid waiting for us.

I shook my head at Lizzy. "What are you doing here?"

She let me know our spies had discovered Moho held Mimi captive as well. I froze. Mimi must be somewhere close-by. I turned on my heel to head back but Kele snagged my arm.

His eyes stern, allowing no argument. "We figure dis out in Avalon. Time to go, now."

CHAPTER 8

MOHO MANO

SHARK

Anger surged through my veins as I swam alongside Nikko, refusing to admit Kupua had eluded us once again. Nikko's twenty-foot, muscular form matched my every motion, gliding and slicing through water, the perfect bodyguard. Together we'd defeat Kupua, but it didn't look like we'd have that chance today. After pursuing him into open ocean, we'd lost track of his scent. Even Nikko, an experienced hunter, had no sense of which direction he'd taken or what form he might have assumed.

My mood darkened and Nikko's focus sharpened, hunger spurring him into a frenzy. My hand stroked his sandpaper skin, the bond between us stronger than a mother and child and our emotions forever linked. After several deep breaths we both calmed enough to maintain control, like a pair of cocked guns ready to fire.

Surface dwellers viewed sharks as killers, but I knew they were intelligent, with complex social relationships based on size and dominance. Smaller sharks gave way to their larger brothers during a feed, demonstrating respect. Like any other predator, sharks hunted for food, never killing needlessly but excelling at survival at the top of the food chain.

Tiger sharks like Nikko exuded power, something I respected and craved. Power hummed through my core, infusing me with the strength of my sharks. From the moment I entered the water, my spirit linked to theirs, sharing knowledge and skills; all increasing in ability. If only I could change form, then this game with Kupua would be over and I could take my place as king.

Smaller tigers trailed Nikko and I, pulsing power forward like a tidal wave surging through the sea, feeding me a constant energy jolt and setting my nerves on fire. Every distinct scent traveling through the ocean cataloged in my brain like an all-you-can-eat buffet. Pulses of electricity hummed through the water on a variety of frequencies, beckoning me to investigate. Instinct warred with cunning as I determined what to do next in my battle for Moku-ola.

Fish parted in front of Nikko and I, creating an open path with no resistance. I swung a leg over Nikko and rolled onto his back, wrapping my arms around his thick body and leaning forward. We swooped as one down through rock arches along the sandy bottom of the sea floor, tingling with awareness of every movement, scent and change in our surroundings. As we glided along the ocean's floor, a shadow loomed above, catching our attention. With a whoosh of his caudal fin, Nikko shot toward the surface, the hunt thrilling through his mind, quickening my heartbeat. We exploded out of the water, a seal gripped in Nikko's jaws, blood spreading out like a cloud, its metallic scent sparking desire deep in my soul. Submerging, Nikko devoured his prize, and within seconds we were deep in the sea, with both our thirst for prey and hunger satiated. Small mako sharks lunged forward to capture stray chunks of meat left in Nikko's wake. Frenzied fighting broke out for a brief moment, before larger reef sharks re-established the pecking order.

Logic, reason and emotions gave sway to instinct, allowing me to shed all humanity and fully connect with my sharks. Emptiness swallowed my thoughts. No distractions, only acute awareness of every scent, every movement, every shadow. Nothing escaped my notice. True power. Farther out to sea we searched, inspecting deeper and wider for any sign of Kupua, but found nothing. He'd done something to mask his scent.

A splash resonated from the surface, capturing Nikko's attention and bringing with it an unusual, musty, bitter scent. Curious, we spun toward the shafts of light brightening the murky depths. Shapes attracted my gaze, dark shadows eclipsing the sun's rays, moving and splashing above us. Voices followed, someone shouted, words mumbling together without forming sense, then a deep, throaty bark. Nikko tensed for attack, building speed and anticipation, but I restrained him, concerned for his safety around surface dwellers who often carried weapons. Screams trilled the air with warning as it became clear Nikko's form had been spotted. Piercing shots sliced through water, leaving trails of bubbles in their wake. I knew the danger of bullets and twisted my body, forcing Nikko to dive, avoiding the tiny missiles streaming through the sea. We didn't need more trouble right now and finding Kupua remained my top priority.

But Kupua would not be found this day. Reluctantly, I steered toward the cave at Two Harbors, directing my fury towards Eka who deserved the blame for Kupua's escape. Her interruption had distracted me, allowing Kele to enter unnoticed and free my brother of his chains. Her actions represented the true cause of the day's failure. Nikko's interest in her flesh as dinner sparked, but my mind rebelled. "No Nikko, she's not for you. She belongs to me."

Ripples spread out like a fan with our arrival at the cavern pool. I heaved my body onto the ledge where events had unfolded earlier and dumped a bucket of squid into the pool, feeding Nikko's growing hunger from the journey and distance we'd covered. Blood and chunks of meat splashed my feet, drenching me with the aroma of chum and causing my stomach to growl with its own hunger. Henry met me, his face solemn.

"Moho, where have you been? We've got issues here."

I spun on him, tensing and he stumbled back a few steps, throwing his hands forward.

"Whoa. Easy there, didn't mean to upset you. I know who's boss, but I've got to report, Sam's gone. He must have run while we were dealing with the others." He paced back and forth. "We don't need him anyway, he's always been weak, caring about others and trying to be nice."

A growl rumbled in my chest. "Where's Eka?"

Henry paled. "I locked her in your room. She's pretty messed up. Maybe we should send her home, she's holding us back. If it wasn't for her we'd still have your loser brother."

My fists clenched as I considered throwing him to Nikko for the mess he'd made. He was just as worthless as his brother, but I needed him. He was the only one who could play the flute. "Leave her to me, you worry about keeping your promise." No way was anyone else leaving my control. Eka belonged to me, no matter how weak and unstable she might be, she remained mine.

Trudging toward my room, I dreaded the moment Eka's voice would grate across my eardrums, shrill and whiny. At first, I thought she'd be useful, make Tessa jealous, but that hadn't worked. Now I kept her around to show I could, and every once in a while she surprised me. Her presence took the sting out of being rejected by Tessa. Arrogant, righteous, Tessa. She did have courage, had to give her that, and beauty. It was clear why she'd been chosen queen.

When I opened the door the stink of charcoal accosted my senses. Eka sprung from a chair in the corner, shaking, her hand waving a piece of paper, face red from crying. Why was she always crying? I grit my teeth and braced myself.

She flung her body at my feet, wrapping her arms around my ankles, her wet cheeks sliding against my calves like slimy chunks of raw fish. "I'm so sorry Moho, I didn't know it was an act until Henry

67

explained it all to me. I should never have doubted you, please don't be mad. I'll make it up to you, I promise."

I flinched. "Get up. If you can't handle who I am maybe you should leave."

Her voice spiked, shrill and loud. "Noooooo. Don't send me away." She shoved a piece of paper in the air. "Here, I made you a drawing, just the way you like."

I snatched the paper from her, examining her work. A charcoal drawing of Nikko capturing every detail of his beauty and grace danced on the page, each line exquisitely drawn, creating the illusion of movement. Eka's drawing showed talent, one of her redeeming qualities. Talent always had uses.

I hopped backwards shaking my leg to liberate myself of her grasp. "Hmmmph. Not bad. I'll accept your apology, but remember, I cannot have you interfering again, understand? You cost me a great deal today."

She stood, wiping her face, leaving black smudges on her cheeks. "Of course. It won't happen again Moho."

"Good." I reached out and pulled her into a hug, releasing her before she became too comfortable. "Once I'm king, everyone will know of your talent. But now, I have a job for you."

Her face lit, red blotches clearing as her mood shifted. At times I even thought her pretty with her curly ringlets and bright eyes.

"Get a bucket of fish and feed our captive, we're going to need her."

Worry clouded her eyes as she bit her fingernails. "But the Lua Pele hole is in there, what if she pushes me into it? You know how much that thing freaks me out. Can't Henry feed her?"

Unbelievable. I shot her a scowl, my anger rising. "Haven't we been over this? If you don't want to help me, then leave. I've got no patience for cowards."

She ducked her head, swiveled on her heels and shuffled out the door without another word, kicking it closed behind her.

CHAPTER 9

MOHO PU'UWAI

EMOTION

Finally, some quiet. Tossing Eka's drawing on a table, I reclined on the bed, reviewing the events of the day. Blood throbbed in my veins, longing for the cool brush of currents against my skin. The hum of my sharks' thoughts a permanent backdrop in my brain like white noise you could never shut off. This makeshift room didn't even offer access to the ocean, with its iron door and stone floor, it reeked of surface when I yearned for salty sea.

Somehow I'd lost focus long enough to allow Kele to ambush my plans. How had that happened? He'd snuck among my sharks without being noticed. It must be Eka, she posed too much of a distraction, took too much energy to pacify and control. I kicked at blankets, heat burning like an inferno in my chest. Sharks were much easier companions, their emotions clear and simple, never leaving one with doubts. They respected dominance, never needed words of encouragement.

Ever since I'd discovered my gift, my ability to control sharks, dominance drove me like a hammer pounding a nail. Without maintaining control, my life would be lost and I would become chum for all ocean predators. Nobody understood the delicate balance of leadership among sharks. Weakness translated into death, and lack of control meant weakness in my world. Memories of the day I'd learned this critical lesson flooded and haunted my mind; the day sharks tore a friend of mine to pieces because of my weakness. Visions of blood and terror on my friend's face haunted me. Never again would I be weak.

Straightening in frustration, I pounded my fists against my thighs. It was time to demonstrate my power, time to use every tool at my disposal, starting with my captive. No more playing nice.

Rising, I stretched my muscles, tensing and releasing until every move was loose and flowing. On dry land emptiness clung to me, a longing only satisfied by immersing myself in the sea among my sharks. In their company I experienced moments of relief in which I no longer felt the sting of loneliness, however fleeting.

I scented Eka, tossing fish to my prisoner, her fear dissipating far too much for my liking. I stalked to the lowest section of my cavern home, determined to rectify the situation. Tunnels here served as hallways, which, if you believed legends, were once traversed by mighty queens of the sea, traveling to secure safety for creatures throughout the oceans.

I opened the door to discover Eka in a far corner, hand-feeding that sea lion Tessa cared so much about, the stench of fish heavy in the air. She actually had a smile on her face. Not what I'd had in mind when I ordered her to complete this task. My fists clenched at my side, itching to slam something. Eka's gaze shot in my direction, her smile fading. Good. I strode over to where she crouched.

"Why are you still here? You were to feed the animal, not befriend her. Just dump the food and go."

Her fingers released the bucket, sending it clanging along the floor, spilling fish and squid. She stood, her eyes averted. "I was just doing what you told me. Why are you mad again?"

"I told you to feed her, *not* entertain her. This is not your pet." Was I really standing here arguing with a girl about feeding a sea lion? Blood boiled in my veins. "LEAVE...NOW."

She pivoted, then paused in mid motion, her voice trembling. "Moho, you are always telling me to leave, always shouting. When can we spend time together? We used to have fun together...do you remember?"

In some distant memory I did remember having fun with her but it seemed a lifetime ago, before she had become an annoying pawn in my plan. Fun had no place in my life now, not until a crown sat on my head. Moku-ola hung in front of me like a present I'd waited too long to open. I raised my hand to shove Eka and a blur knocked me sideways, teeth clamping onto my arm.

"Mimmmi, noooooooo!" Eka screamed.

72

I corrected my balance, pain stabbing through my arm like a hot poker. Gripping Mimi's jaw with my free hand, I squeezed until she released my flesh. Blood oozed from a torn and jagged wound, dripping onto the floor, triggering my instincts for defense. With my now free hand I latched onto a flipper and heaved her across the room, watching her spiral away from me with satisfaction.

Eka lunged toward the sea lion as she catapulted into the air, colliding mid-way, sending them both skidding along the ground toward the Lua Pele hole. I leapt toward Eka and snatched her leg before she plummeted over the side, barely catching her in time, yanking her back from the abyss. Mimi let out a howl as she tumbled over the edge and into the lair of the Lua Pele.

Tears spilled down Eka's face as she dropped her head into her hands and sobbed. I released her leg and stood, brushing slimy bits of fish and bones off my shins. Once again Eka had cost me a valuable tool against Tessa and my brother. Why had I bothered to save her? I poked her with my foot. "Get up."

She struggled to her knees and pleaded at me with red puffy eyes. I held out my hand and she clutched it, pulling herself to her feet, maintaining eye contact as she straightened. "That sea lion was only protecting me. She didn't deserve to die. Why would you throw her down there?"

"No one sinks their teeth in me and lives. You're lucky I didn't let you go with her."

She rubbed her eyes, taking a deep breath. "Why didn't you?"

Good question, but not one I wanted to answer. Between Eka, Henry and Sam, I felt exhausted from babysitting, longing for the days when Nikko and I traversed the waters alone, hunting in the deep. Humans were making me soft. I whirled away from her, stalking towards the door. "Next time I might not be so generous. Don't forget it."

CHAPTER 10

TESSA

CATALINA

Crowds of people jammed the streets of Avalon, music from a jazz festival blaring in the background, mixing with the steady hum of conversations and laughter. Steel drums vibrated on a corner thrumming out an enticing beat, inviting some to dance on street corners, throwing their hands in the air with abandon. Yachts crowded the bay, tied to dinghies floating on the surface, gently swaying with the waves. Water taxis shuttled groups of people back and forth from the dock, packed like sardines within their narrow hulls. Sea gulls swarmed overhead in the crystal blue sky, hunting for unsuspecting tourists foolish enough to leave food unattended. No one blinked an eye as we swam ashore, leaving Lizzy and Sid waiting near Lover's Cove, about a mile away.

Kupua planned to meet us on the pier so we wove our way through the mass of surface dwellers to set up watch nearby. Cotton candy and waffle cones released enticing scents wafting in the breeze, triggering hunger pangs in my stomach.

"Hey, what do you say we grab some food when Kupua gets here? Anyone else hungry?" I asked, patting my stomach.

Kele burst into a grin. "Great idea. You da bomb. I'm always down fo' some grinds my queen."

Akalei rubbed his round stomach. "We know." He chuckled and pulled her into a hug.

"Eh, naff awready. You know you love yo big macoon husband. Mo fo' love." She squeezed him back, planting a kiss on his cheek. I smiled and quickened my pace, giving them a moment alone as we walked along the boardwalk. Their love witnessed to me how two people strengthened one another, coaxing out the best in each.

We plopped down at the end of the pier and dangled our legs off the edge, scanning the swells for any sign of Kupua. Bright orange Garibaldi fish nipped at my toes playfully, tickling my skin. Placing my hands on the warm wooden planks of the dock, I leaned back and absorbed the carefree atmosphere, enjoying a short reprieve from nonstop action of the past few days, well maybe longer than a few days. Exhaling, tension evaporated off my shoulders as I slumped back farther against the pier. It wasn't long before Kupua thrust his hand out of the water and hauled himself onto the dock, shaking water from his head and spraying us with cool droplets.

The worry clutching my heart released and I let out a sigh, wrapping my arms around his neck and leaning my head into his damp chest, grateful he'd made it back safely. I licked salty drops from his hair off my lips, inhaling the fresh smell of the sea wafting off his skin. His comfort and reassurance poured into my soul, chasing out all worries.

Kele broke the silence. "Hey brah, wat took so long? We hungry."

Kupua laughed, flicking water in Kele's direction. "You're always hungry Kele. What's new?"

Kele's eyes widened as if he was surprised. "Fo'real?"

"Yeah, fo'real. Better get food before there's real trouble." Kupua snagged my hand and strolled down the pier, dripping water as he walked. Kele and Akalei scrambled to follow.

Kupua tipped his head in my direction. "Any requests?"

"With Kele to feed, I think we should go for quantity, not quality."

He threw his head back and laughed, shooting a glance behind us at his friend. His laughter helped put life into perspective for me, reminding me nothing trumped love of the Creator and each other, we were meant to have joy and fun, always appreciating our time together. Moho would never take love from us, could never steal or destroy the camaraderie we shared. My heart stung for Moho's pain and I held onto hope he could feel our love someday and return to his place with our family.

We ducked into a small taco stand and positioned ourselves at the bar, Kele took one look at the menu and ordered everything on it. With a glint in his eye, Kupua gently shoved his shoulder. "What, just one of everything, why stop there, how about two?"

Kele patted his stomach. "My wahine has me on da diet."

"Like that's possible," Akalei chirped as she slid onto a barstool and downed an icy glass of water.

With the concert outside in full swing, the place had emptied, leaving us alone to spread out, although the tiny restaurant didn't have much room to start with, crammed with booths and a plastic, life-size fake fish welcoming patrons at the door. Mobiles of driftwood and shells hung from the ceiling, adding to its seaside charm. Of course, size hardly mattered when you were known for amazing food and soon sizzling platters of tacos and fajitas kept our attention as we satiated our ravenous hunger.

The soft jingle of the bell over the door rang as someone entered the tiny restaurant. Kupua tensed next to me and I glanced over my shoulder to find Sam lurking in the doorway, wringing his hands and looking frazzled. Kupua and Kele both stood, maneuvering themselves between us. Sam immediately threw his shaking hands in the air.

"Hey, I'm not here to cause trouble. I want to help you. There's some stuff you need to know."

Kupua's voice rumbled a low growl. "Why would you help us?"

Sam's head drooped, his shoulders slumping as he stared at his feet as if they might answer on his behalf. "I never wanted to hurt anyone. Helping Moho was my brother's idea, but we had no idea what he was capable of and now Henry's in too deep. I have to figure out how to stop all this, how to get him away from Moho." He

78

looked at us. "Please, I know you don't trust me, but at least listen to what I have to say."

Kupua bent to whisper in my ear. "Tessa, this is your decision. What do you want to do?"

I paused and met Sam's eyes, searching his soul for confirmation of what I already suspected. Sorrow and compassion stirred within him, deep pools reflecting in his brown eyes. I rose and moved closer to Sam, placing my hand on his shoulder. "I believe you don't want to hurt us. We will listen to what you have to say and then decide what to do."

Sam covered my hand with his and his eyes softened with appreciation. "Thank you."

I nodded. "Is there somewhere more private we can talk? This isn't the right place for the conversation we need to have."

Sam straightened. "I have a ranch not far from here. It's private and we'd be alone. My jeep's just outside."

I inclined my head towards the door. "Okay, let's go."

Akalei leaned against me, putting her mouth near my ear. "Are you sure we should trust him Tessa?"

"No, but I believe he's telling us the truth and we don't have any other leads right now. Besides, he might reveal something useful and we sure could use any information at this point." Kupua and Kele just shook their heads and followed us out the door, but not before Kele grabbed a taco 'to go' off his plate.

We squeezed into Sam's jeep, just barely. I sat up front while Kupua, Kele and Akalei crammed into the back seat. The sun shone high in the sky and wind whipped my face as we cruised high into the hills of Avalon Canyon in Sam's open-air ride. I lifted my hands, savoring the warm air blowing against my skin, reminding me of younger days when I'd ride with my mom along the coast in her convertible singing out loud to her favorite oldies station. Eucalyptus trees lined the street, their aroma drifting along the breeze. Sun beat on my face and I closed my eyes in bliss.

Sam's ranch sprawled for acres, nestled in the hills above Avalon. Mares with foals grazed among grassy fields, accompanied by the occasional collie, patrolling the perimeter. We turned onto a dirt road and jostled away from the main highway, every bump bouncing us off our seats. Kele grunted as one bump bounced his head into the bar overhead.

"Dat hurt brah, be mo careful."

Kupua tossled his hair. "No harm done, your head's too thick. Probably won't even have a bump."

Kele jerked his head away from Kupua's hand and frowned. Behind us billows of dust rose, marking our progress along the dusty road.

Sam's modest one-story house set back among the trees was surrounded by flower gardens bursting with color. Red, pink and white geraniums lined the stone walkway to his front door, welcoming us.

We jerked to a stop in front and I bounced out of the jeep, stretching my legs and absorbing the peaceful setting, inhaling the aroma of flowers, earth and eucalyptus. Kupua brushed loose strands of hair from my face, his own hair in windy disarray.

"You miss the open air."

I shrugged. "Sometimes." I touched his cheek, giving him my most reassuring smile. "But I don't regret a moment of my life in Moku-ola."

He tilted his head, his dimples puckering as he smiled. "We'll have to visit here often."

Akalei and Kele jumped out from the back of the jeep and joined us, Kele rubbing his head and walking stiffly like an old man who'd been sitting too long.

"Getting too old for adventures Kele?" Kupua shouted over my head.

Akalei linked her arm in mine. "If you're coming back here, don't forget how much I love an adventure and Kele enjoys hanging out at the surface. You have to bring us along."

Kele brightened at her statement. "Befo' time I always visit da surface."

Gratefulness bubbled in my heart, pressing tears of joy against the back of my eyes. No matter where life took me, if they were by my side, I'd be okay.

Sam pointed toward the house. "We can sit out on the back patio, this way." He led us around to the back of the house where a flagstone patio stretched into the trees. A pond teaming with giant, spotted Koi curled around the far corner of the patio in an L shape. We each took a seat in padded chairs displaying patterns of yellow sunflowers, set in a circle and settled in. Kele sighed as he wiggled to find a comfy position, glaring at me when I giggled at his efforts.

"Sorry Kele, but wimp much?"

"Wot? I be no wimp, dis chair just da bomb aftah dat jeep ride."

"That's right sweetie, you tell her," Akalei clucked, sneaking me a wink.

Sam disappeared into the house and returned with a tray of glasses and a pitcher of lemonade. After serving everyone he eased into one of the chairs, letting out a sigh of his own.

I narrowed my gaze at him. "Okay, we're listening."

Sam leaned in, elbows on his knees, hands folded together. "My brother and I are the only surviving descendants of a royal lineage fallen from power long ago. The flute Moho seeks to control has been in our family for decades, but until now none of us have played it, aware it released an evil capable of great destruction. You search for the reason why fish are dying…it's the flute."

Kupua and I exchanged a glance, he'd just confirmed what we already suspected but hadn't been able to prove. "How do we stop it?" I asked.

Sam shook his head. "You can't. You can only stop Moho from using Henry to play it, and Henry is loyal to Moho, don't ask me why, but he is. The flute opens a portal to the depths of the underworld and looses the players' chosen destruction." He paused and ran his trembling hand through his hair. "I don't understand why, but Henry won't listen to me, he's determined to help Moho. I've never seen him like this, it's like he's changed, no longer the brother I grew up with. We've always been able to talk to each other, but not anymore. Now, all he hears is Moho." Pain etched his features, the estrangement from his brother cost him.

Sounded familiar. Seemed we now had two errant brothers on the loose.

"A portal?" I choked on the word. How does one close off a portal to the underworld? My chest tightened. This revelation brought new dimensions and urgency to our quest.

He waved away my statement. "That's not all I wanted to tell you. Henry's discovered another weapon. It's called a weather spear and whoever possesses it controls the power of the elements. He hasn't given it to Moho yet and keeps it hidden at his estate."

He paused, wringing his hands and clearing his throat. "I know I have no right to ask anything of you but I have one favor to request. I'm really worried about Eka. She's only a child and doesn't realize Moho's using her, and I believe she's in real danger. I don't know how things have gotten so out of control, but Moho's getting more desperate and violent. Promise me you'll get her out of there, take her to safety and I'll tell you how to find someone else you're looking for."

I narrowed my eyes at him. "Don't play with us Sam. We'll try to help Eka, but she has to make her own choices. We won't kidnap or force her. Now…who do you think we're looking for?"

His hands fell into his lap, grief and defeat etched in the lines of his face. "I've been told you search for a sea lion named Mimi, is that correct?"

I leaned forward. "Yes." Kupua tensed next to me. Sam didn't seem to notice.

"Moho is holding her prisoner in the same cavern he trapped you in. She's sick and won't make it long. I'm so sorry, I wish I could have done more to help."

Kele and Akalei let out a gasp. We'd suspected Mimi might be held captive in that location but this confirmation erased all doubts.

"What does Moho want with her? Why did he take her?" After all, he hadn't mentioned her when he held us in chains or used her captivity to gain my agreement to marry him.

Sam looked at his hands and shrugged. "Moho and Henry didn't tell me much about their plans. Henry just asked me to help them, I wasn't there long before you arrived. I wouldn't have gone at all if I hadn't been so worried about Henry. Being under the water freaks me out." His expression pleaded with me. "Henry's a good brother, he's not all bad and I don't want to lose him. Promise me you won't hurt him, that you'll give him a chance."

"I can't promise you anything, but I do believe people can change; make a choice to do the right thing. I won't give up on Henry."

I straightened and considered my friends, knowing what we had to do next, hoping they'd agree. Kupua nodded, strengthening my resolve. I studied Kele and Akalei, fully understanding the risk I was about to ask them to take, confident they would face it with courage and announced, "We have to go back."

CHAPTER 11

HO'I HOU

RETURN

Driving along the bumpy road toward Avalon, my mind wandered, wondering what precipitated two very different brothers to fall so far astray and even more importantly, what might lead them back to their families? Of course, I had some experience with this topic on a personal level. I'd done my own straying after my parents' accident and hadn't been such a great sister to Rachel before discovering my own true purpose and worth in life. Accepting forgiveness transformed my heart, forever altering the course my life had taken. I ached for Moho to experience the joy and freedom I'd found, to be released from the prison of his pain and self-loathing.

I jerked when Kupua leaned forward and tapped my shoulder. He brushed my hair with his lips as he whispered in my ear. "Hey, you seem pretty lost in thought, everything okay?"

Craning my neck around to peer at him, I spoke into the

wind. "Yeah. Just trying to figure out how to get through to Moho and Henry. There has to be a way, right?"

"There's always hope, Tessa." He sounded confident, but I spied the flicker of doubt slip across his expression as he shifted his eyes away and it broke my heart. Had he given up on his brother?

I shoved all my determination into my next words. "You'll have your brother back Kupua, someday, somehow. I'll never give up on him."

He dropped his chin on my shoulder, hiding his face and I barely caught his next words. "Let's just pray it's before he destroys anyone else."

Sam dumped us off near Lover's Cove where we sat cross-legged on gravel to patch together some semblance of a plan. Lover's Cove served as a popular snorkeling spot and protected underwater park, rife with popular, bright orange, Garibaldi fish. This late in the day, as the sun dipped below the horizon, it had cleared out and was far enough from town to give us some privacy.

Lizzy lumbered onto the gravel and plopped her head in my lap. She rubbed her wet nose against my leg and whimpered concern about Mimi, urging us to hurry. I ran my hands across her sleek wet fur, cupping her muzzle and planting a kiss on top of her nose, gagging a bit at her rank breath. "We've got to get you some mouthwash, sweetie. Do you have news for us?"

She did. Moho reportedly was out searching for Kupua and had ventured far enough into the open ocean Sid believed we could get in and out of his hideaway before he returned. Finally, a break.

About time something went our way.

Kupua raised an eyebrow, out of water he wasn't able to hear her thoughts. I cleared my throat. "She says Moho's pretty far away right now but no word on Henry. This might be our best opportunity to sneak inside his hideout and rescue Mimi, but we need to hustle."

Kupua rose. "Okay, then I vote we get over there and bring Mimi home."

Kele moaned, shaking his head. "Brah, Tessa and Akalei should stay here wit Lizzy, keep safe."

I rolled my eyes at him. "Do we have to replay this conversation again? Kele we've been over this. I'm queen, this is my responsibility."

Akalei shoved between us, interrupting. "Kele, we stay together and take care of each other, that's the deal, remember. We have each other's backs. No way I'm hanging here while you and Kupua risk your lives."

He threw his hands in the air, pleading with Kupua who shook his head, pity etched on his face. "They're right Kele, we're in this together. We go as a team. Besides, you know Tessa and Akelei. They'd never relax here, waiting for us. You *have* met them."

Kele closed his eyes, covering his face with his hands. "Kay den, going going."

I reached over and rubbed his back. "Akalei and I'll be careful, and we'll get Mimi and get out, easy peasy." I didn't bother reminding him, our plans never seemed to be simple or easy. He'd learned that lesson firsthand.

CHAPTER 12

HO'OPAKELE

RESCUE

We arrived back at the pool where we'd last seen Moho and Henry thrashing among sharks. As we sprung from water onto the ledge, our wet feet splat against rock, echoing off the walls. No one, not even a shark remained to welcome us. I crept to the door Eka had burst from earlier and pressed my ear against its cold, damp iron, hearing only the drip of water seeping through cracks in its seam. Maybe they'd all left and, thank the Creator, we might actually pull this escape off. I really didn't want more drama with Henry or Moho today – *way* past my quota for a lifetime.

Kupua pounded his shoulder into the iron door until it creaked open, revealing a hall with a door on one side and a passageway on the other. I squeezed past Kupua and crept into the passage. It sloped downward, dark and foreboding. We snuck down the hall, venturing deeper into Moho's lair, hugging the wall and rubbing our arms as the air grew chilly. It was like walking into a meat locker. My breath puffed into clouds, misting the air. The passage ended at a small wooden door hung on rusty hinges and slightly ajar. Inside someone sobbed. Slowly, carefully, I peered around the door, holding my breath with hope Henry wasn't crouching on the other side.

Eka huddled against the far wall, head in her hands, oblivious to our presence. Faint bruises blossomed yellow and orange under her skin along one arm. She wore a crumpled t-shirt with a ripped hem, stained and filthy, hanging over black leggings. I tiptoed over to her, keeping low to the ground so as not to startle her, hand over my mouth in an attempt to block the retched smell of sulfur and death permeating the room. I squatted next to her and spoke softly. "Eka, it's Tessa. Are you okay?"

She mumbled into her hands, not bothering to lift her head. "You must hate me, Tessa. Just leave me alone, Moho will be back soon and you don't want to be here when he returns. I know you think he's bad but he cares about me."

"Eka, I don't hate you, I want to help you. Will you come with us home to Moku-ola?"

She shook her head violently. "No, I can't, Moho will be mad if I leave. He told me to wait here. I have to stay here."

Kele inched forward but I waved him back. Eka clearly wasn't ready to deal with anyone and I doubted she'd let Kele examine her. "Eka, do you know where Mimi's being held?"

Her body shook and sobbing started again. "Moho...got

mad…and threw…her into…" She pointed to a hole in the corner; a Lua Pele hole.

My heart sunk, expecting the worst, but hoping Eka remembered wrong. Kupua quickly strode to the hole and leaned in, calling out Mimi's name. I scrambled over to him, scrutinizing the darkness, jagged stone cutting into my hands as I gripped the side of the hole. I gagged on the stench of sulfur and rotting flesh rolling from the depths of emptiness below.

A soft whimper answered us. I held out my arm, lighting the black void with my wristband. Mimi sat wedged on a small rock ledge not far from the top of the hole. My heart jumped in my throat, beyond excited she lived. Cuts streaked across her side and back, blood oozing down her flippers, but she was alive! Her head drooped as she whimpered and blinked at the light shining in her eyes.

Kele unwound rope from his pack, forming a loop and lowering it, sliding the noose across her body, catching behind her flippers. She whined.

Agony and pain consumed her and she didn't want to move. I told her we needed to get her out, take her home, doing my best to soothe her ragged nerves. Kele and Kupua both gripped the rope and tugged, gently lifting her off the ledge toward us. Her whimpers tore at me like daggers. When she cleared the hole I threw my arms around her, hugging her close, her head falling against my chest and blood smearing my skin. Kele kneeled next to me and wrapped her wounds, preparing her for the trip home. Taking his time, he cooed into her ear as he worked. I glanced back at Eka who watched from her corner, confused and alone.

"She's alive. How can that be?" Eka squeaked.

I released my hold on Mimi and scooted toward her. "She landed on a ledge and didn't fall too deep into the hole. Who knows what would've happened if we hadn't gotten here when we did." By the look of her condition she wouldn't have been able to stay on the ledge for much longer. I didn't want to think about having to tell Lizzy bad news.

Eka sniffed, coiling her arms around her legs and curling into a ball.

"Eka, please come home with us. We can't leave you here, you're hurt." I reached out and touched her bruised face.

She flinched, pain and sorrow swirling in her eyes, breaking my heart.

Akalei sat down next to us, a drawing in her hand. "Hey Eka, did you draw this?" She spread the paper out so we all could see, an intricate, detailed depiction of Moho swimming with his sharks. She nodded her head. I traced the drawing with my finger, admiring how she'd captured his mood so well.

"This is really good Eka, you're very talented."

She raised her head slightly, revealing the beginning of a smile. "Thanks. Moho says I am, too. It's the only thing I really love to do."

Akalei gently laid her hand on Eka's shoulder. "Would you come back with us, just for a little while? Tessa's been wanting more art displayed in the city, we could exhibit some of your work and

91

maybe you could help the younger children develop their talent more." I repressed the urge to hug Akalei for being so brilliant, and nodded in agreement at Eka.

A spark ignited in Eka's face, the slightest sliver of hope, and I sucked in my breath praying we'd swayed her enough to return.

"Do you really think it's good enough to display, Tessa?"

"Absolutely. You would honor me if you'd consider doing this. I'd consider it a personal favor."

She shrugged her shoulders. "I guess I could come back for a little while. Moho's not here that much anyway. Promise you'll let me come back if I want to."

"Yes, we promise. Just return for a little while, long enough to get an art show going. Thank you, Eka." Akalei and I helped her to her feet, our strength bolstering her as she faltered, her legs shaking. Kele fashioned a sling around Mimi to pull her behind us once in the water. My nerves tingled as I hopped from one foot to another. Moho wasn't going to be happy when he discovered both Mimi and Eka vanished from under his nose. I wanted us long gone before that scenario played out.

Kupua and Kele gently toted Mimi between them, back to water. Akalei and I trailed on either side of Eka as she limped up the incline to the entrance of the hideaway. We held hands with her as we slipped into the water, grateful no sharks had yet returned.

Once we'd put a few miles between us and Moho's hideaway, the tension drained from my muscles, a significant lead deceiving me into a sense of security. I knew it was only a matter of time before he'd realize what we'd done and give chase.

Currents ran in our favor, sweeping us back toward the Hawaiian Islands much faster than our trip out. Despite making good time, we'd have to find a place to sleep for the night. Kupua and Sid swam ahead, scouting locations for our overnight stay. Kele trailed him, towing Mimi and staying closer to the surface to allow her air breaks. Akalei and I lagged behind the group with Eka between us, traveling slower to allow for her weakened state.

Warning voices blared through my head; oceanic alarms from surrounding fish, alerting me to something approaching from deep below. *Danger*, they screamed, over and over, crying for me to flee. Lack of visibility prevented me from seeing anything amiss, but I trusted my friends of the sea. I motioned to Akalei we needed to catch up to the others or find a more defensible spot. Her eyes widened with fear and she reached out to clutch my arm and draw close. Resisting, I kicked in reverse, waving my hand at her to swim away.

Kupua caught the alarm in my mind but he'd gotten too far ahead to double-back and get to us in time. Barracuda surrounded me, attempting to camouflage my presence. Eka sensed the change and nervously scanned the sea, her eyes darting back and forth. Akalei stroked her arm, cooing encouraging words in her ear, all the while refusing to acknowledge my demand that she and Eka flee.

Between masses of fish I caught a glimpse of shapes emerging from below. Moho swam among them, riding anger as a wave, announcing his pending arrival. I distanced myself further from Akalei and Eka. Akalei twisted in the water, glaring at me with panic in her eyes. I shook my head at her, waving her forward to get Eka to safety. She paused, indecision etched on her features, but I couldn't have Eka in danger, not when we'd just rescued her. "Get Eka out of here now Akalei, I'm ordering you. It's up to you to keep her safe." Every ounce of authority I possessed I injected into my voice.

Resignation mingled with sadness for a moment in Akalei's eyes before she hugged Eka tight against her body and sped away, leaving me alone in her wake. I watched her retreat, praying I'd bought them enough time to reach somewhere safe.

Hovering in the water, I faced the oncoming mass of bodies, bracing myself as I trembled. Moho led the army atop a massive tiger shark, the two moving as one, as if the shark were an extension of his body, gliding through the sea in perfect synchronization. Swallowing, I shoved fear aside. Sharks swept past mere inches from my flesh, their movement generating a wave of pressure tingling across my skin. Each mind I explored seemed razor sharp but constrained with a membrane like barrier, controlled by an outside force. Moho's signature imprinted on their minds unmistakable.

A hand captured my ankle, yanking me down, careening toward the bottom, biting into my skin with enough force to rip a cry from my throat. Water churned as fish and barracuda nipped at sharks, frantic to help, their fear thick as molasses. I ordered them to stop, directing them to safety. Even barracudas didn't stand a chance against Moho's sharks and I couldn't live with their deaths on my shoulders. I may not be able to fight sharks but I could at least protect my friends. I forced my muscles to go limp and allowed Moho to drag me down, reaching out to the Creator and putting my trust in His protection.

As we neared the sea floor, a familiar hole came into view – the largest Lua Pele hole I'd ever seen. Muscles clenched as fear skidded across my every nerve. Moho didn't slow, he raced straight for the opening. I fought bile as it rose in my throat, resisting the urge to fight against his hold on my leg. Everything in me screamed not to enter that lair, but I knew it was futile, his hold as strong as an iron manacle and flanked with sharks, my chances for escape were nil. He dove inside, jerking me with him. Darkness enveloped us and I reached out for Kupua, sending him my location, grasping at any hope for rescue. He tracked me, sending warmth to keep my fears at bay, letting me know I wasn't alone. I didn't want him tracking me into this pit, but Moho hadn't given me much choice. Rotting flesh and sulfur overwhelmed my senses, causing me to gag and wretch until my stomach twisted in pain. My wristband lit and I got my first glimpse of why legends had our people fearing the Lua Pele.

CHAPTER 13

HO'IKE

TEST

In the darkest places, the Creator's light shines the brightest. Courage, not borne from myself, strengthened me as I absorbed my surroundings. We'd entered an air lock tunnel and crept through a hot, dank, cramped area. Snakes slithered along the floor, writhing and curling around one another as I leapt over them, forcing back shudders of revulsion. Slime squished through my toes, and I did my best not to think too much about what comprised the gooey mess oozing over my skin. Bits of flesh clung to rocks jutting out of the walls, and I swerved to keep from rubbing against them. Seaweed clogged the passage, hanging in dripping strings from the ceiling, causing me to swipe wildly as we passed through, leaving a slimy residue on my hands. Sweat dripped into my eyes as the temperature rose, creating a sauna in the tight tunnel. Steam sizzled between rock boulders, misting the air into a thick fog. Sulfur stung my nose, reeking of death, as my chest heaved to inhale the heavy, burning air.

Moho grabbed my hands and bound them together with rope, jerking me forward without even a glance in my direction. Rope stung as I twisted my wrists, hoping to loosen the bonds. Great, with my hands bound I couldn't even keep sweat and slime off my face. My eyes blurred but it didn't stop me from boring a hole in Moho's back with my glare as my mind buzzed, trying to figure out how to escape this mess.

It occurred to me submission would be a far more successful tool in this situation than fighting. Moho's soul hung in the balance and somewhere along the way I'd decided to battle for him, to hold out hope he could still be saved, even if he didn't appreciate my efforts.

"I thought no one could survive the Lua Pele? How is it you can travel down here unharmed?"

He didn't miss a step as he spoke, his voice harsh and cold. "There is much you don't understand, Tessa. Be quiet and observe."

I didn't like the sound of that. My skin tingled with awareness and knowledge that something watched us. Dread pressed upon my shoulders, whispering lies into my ear. *I wasn't good enough to be queen. No one really loved or cared for me. I didn't know what I was doing.* Each lie embedded in a kernel of my own doubt; doubt I'd put aside when I'd accepted the Creator's gift and became queen. Why were they returning now? I reached out for Kupua but something blocked my thoughts, an unseen barrier I couldn't penetrate no matter how I strained to make contact.

Moho snickered as I stumbled, falling on my bound hands, scraping my knees on rocks hidden beneath slime. Pausing, gravel digging into my palms, red scratches covering my legs, I struggled to resist the pull of despair. Heaviness blanketed me, even as my spirit fought against it, calling out to my Creator. Images of battle being waged around me flashed across my vision, quickly lost again to darkness. Was I hallucinating?

Moho yanked me upright, turning his back as soon as I took a step forward. Grey circles under his eyes made him look older, as if his very essence was being sucked from his soul. Shadows flickered ahead and the darkness thickened with a black gloom even my wristbands couldn't penetrate. I tried to focus on what I knew to be true. My family and friends loved me. The Creator had chosen me to be queen. Each thought immediately attacked by an opposing whisper, spitting deceit into my ear.

Moho's voice echoed off the walls, deeper and crueler than normal, no longer his voice but something wicked within, pure evil. His eyes lost all color, shifting to pools of blackness as thick as the evil surrounding us. A mist circled around him, pulsing and breathing with a life of its own. He growled at me. "You failed. You couldn't keep the flute. You allowed fish to be slaughtered. Your friends have abandoned you. Give yourself to me, Tessa, only I can give you the power you need. Power to rule both sea and land."

I shook my head, rebelling against his lies. Or were they? My voice cracked. "Who are you? What do you want?"

Moho shoved his hand against my back and slammed me to my knees, his voice harsh and wrought with anger. "Declare yourself mine and I will answer your questions, give you everything you desire. Crown me your king!"

An icy shadow hovered over me, pressing with the weight of the world. My lungs gasped, burning from inhaling steamy sulfur air. Despair crushed my soul, drowning me in agonizing fear nipping the edges of my mind. I used every ounce of strength within me to resist the temptation to submit and end the torment of resistance.

Moho's voice raked across my senses, like nails on a chalkboard. "No one can help you here, not even your Creator. If you turn yourself over to my care I will transform you into the most powerful queen ever to rule in Moku-ola. Stop fighting and accept your fate."

My spirit recognized deception lacing his words and recoiled, every muscle rejecting his offer. The Creator promised to be always by my side, if only I would keep my eyes on Him. Slowly, carefully, I pushed to my feet, focusing every thought on what I knew to be right, shielding my heart with truth. Power did not belong to me. Power belonged to Him who made me.

Warmth flowed through my veins as love washed over me, lifting the weight of despair. I would never be alone, never rejected, always loved. I squared my shoulders and allowed strength to infuse my voice, looking Moho straight in the eyes. "Your lies have no power over me. You have nothing I desire. You are loved Moho, a treasured member of our family. Please return to Moku-ola with me, your brother wants you back. There will always be a place for you in our city, it is your home, where you belong. Whatever the Lua Pele has promised you, it's a lie and will only lead to destruction."

Darkness shimmered in waves around him like reflections off glass. Something wavered in his eyes, gone in a second, but I'd seen it before emptiness engulfed him. A moment of longing and hope escaped, buried deep in the recesses of his soul. Some part of Moho, wanted to believe me and desired freedom.

He reached above his head and slung the rope binding my wrists through a metal loop hanging from the ceiling. He tied it off in a knot and stepped away, allowing just enough slack in the line for movement. "You've made your choice. Good bye, Tessa." He spun and stalked off, leaving me alone in darkness.

I licked my cracked lips and swallowed, my parched throat swollen and raw. My tongue felt like it had grown three sizes. How I longed for a cool glass of water. My head drooped as I eased myself onto the ground and sat cross-legged in the muck and slime, too exhausted to care about what slithered beneath me. Repeated attempts to contact any of my friends in the sea failed, blocked by the force of hatred barricaded around me.

Kupua's face flashed across my thoughts. My heart yearned for the comfort of his arms, the reassurance of his voice. What if I never saw him again? Never spoke to him again? My soul rebelled at the thought he might not ever hear my words pronounce him king, shout my love for him to the people of Moku-ola. Tears streamed down my face and I captured them with my lips, providing small comfort to my raw throat.

A whisper tickled my ear like a fly buzzing my head, spinning thoughts of self-doubt and insecurity, depressing my spirit. Each time I rejected a thought, it vanished, only to be replaced by another, repeating the process over again, wearing me down bit by bit. Sweat trickled down my face and neck, dampening my hair until it clung against my back.

I drifted in and out of consciousness, possibly for days, since I had no sense of time and night or day made no difference in my new world. My head bobbed forward as a distant light burned through the never-ending night, jolting me awake. My eyes squinted against its brightness, as each beam sent piercing pain shooting through my retinas. The buzzing around my ears stopped, and a strong, booming voice claimed the space in my mind. *Rise, Tessa, leave this place. Your friends are waiting. No evil can hold those who belong to the Creator.*

I trembled at the familiar voice, but didn't stand, fearful I'd finally gone insane. Muscles in my arms and legs cramped, shooting arrows of pain as I shifted my weight in an effort to lean toward the light seeking solace in the peace it offered.

Rope tore and tumbled around my ankles, freeing me from my bonds. I stumbled to my feet, bathed in white light, a beacon amidst despair. Fragrant cinnamon wafted across my senses, filling me with peace, easing the aches of being confined for so long. Intense light urged me forward. I scrambled to respond, stiffly running and slowly waking my reluctant muscles. Basked in light, the way glowing before me, my joy increased with every step, the oppression of darkness lifting off my shoulders. Dawning realization hit as I awakened to the truth behind my newfound freedom, nothing could defeat the plans of my Creator. He held the ultimate authority and power and the Lua Pele merely played at being a cheap imitation. By the time I exploded from the hole, my spirit soared with gratefulness for a release so complete it felt as if I'd spent a week in a spa being pampered like a celebrity.

I shot forward careening into the arms of Kupua, who waited just outside the entrance to the Lua Pele lair. His strong arms hugged me tight as he buried his face in my neck, murmuring with relief. "Thank the Creator you're safe. I thought I'd lost you."

With my cheek pressed against his solid chest, and my arms wrapped around his waist, I clung to the safety he offered. White light wrapped around us both a few moments before fading, leaving us to comfort one another. Emotions crashed over me and I went limp against Kupua, exhausted, shaking and numb. I didn't want to let go…ever.

CHAPTER 14

MOHO
MANA'OLANA

HOPE

How did she do it? For a flicker of time, I'd almost believed I could return home, Tessa's lies tricking me into the possibility of hope. Part of me craved home, family, acceptance, but a stronger part knew those luxuries no longer existed for me in my world. Destiny called me to a greater purpose. That momentary spark she'd ignited snuffed out, choked by familiar despair. I knew where I belonged.

Tessa's deception would not sway me and abandoning her alone in darkness seemed a fitting reward for such treachery. Nothing overpowered the Lua Pele and my pact ensured no chance of escape for Tessa. It also meant I could not refuse a command from my new sovereign, but power never came without a price. By the time I returned for Tessa, she'd be much more cooperative and then we'd see who would claim the crown.

Nikko flicked his tail and dove us into the vast depths of sea so deep no human ever dared explore. Sanctuary. A black void enveloped me, interrupted only by sparks of electrical light illuminating off reclusive fish. Pressure wrapped me like a weighted blanket as we passed one thousand feet, my body now immune to the bone chilling temperatures this far from the sun. Predators ruled in this wilderness and only the strongest survived, something I understood well. Surface dwellers could not conceive what nightmares lurked in these depths. A mammoth man-of-war glided by, streaming stingers floating in its wake, undulating with currents like banners in the wind. I shifted Nikko toward a shaft of red light in the distance. Time to connect with the Lua Pele in its home lair, not Tessa's prison, which served as a mere shadow of the Lua Pele's power.

Glowing ruby rocks lined each side of the cavern's entrance, providing a beacon to guide us to the location. As we approached sacred ground, Nikko slowed, anticipating the prey always waiting for him, a reward from our mysterious host. Squirming on a line set into stone near the entrance of the Lua Pele's home hung two squid, tentacles dangling below their bodies. Stalagmites of salt jutted up from the sea floor like castle pillars as far as the eye could see, the ground desolate and void of any life. No living thing ventured too close to the Lua Pele's home base, unlike me, who had earned immunity and extended it to my sharks.

I released my grip on Nikko as he bolted forward and ripped

squid off the line, shaking his head, leaving a murky cloud of body parts slowly drifting to the sea floor. Scents of blood and death tinged the water, wetting my own appetite. Nikko's satisfaction warmed my blood as I swam through the entrance, anxious for my meeting.

Inside the cave, walls burned red, fueled by volcanic lava, spiking the temperature to an almost unbearable degree. Heat slowed the blood in my veins and a burning sensation built in my lungs. My time communing with the Lua Pele was always limited by the weakness of my flesh. No other fish dared enter the cave, not even my sharks would stray far into this territory.

Smooth, black, polished rock formed a throne against the wall and I took my seat and waited, cursing my own inability to endure for long in such a special place. One never knew how long it might take the Lua Pele to present itself.

Bubbles streamed between crevices as steam released from lava flowing beneath the ground, creating a fog of vapors. I longed for my own release, a time when I would finally be crowned king of Moku-ola, when I would no longer be a fugitive banned from the city of my youth. With allies like the Lua Pele and Henry's flute, success seemed certain.

Water swirled, fizzing and popping, announcing the Lua Pele's arrival. A voice echoed in my ear, hoarse and scratchy.

Brave warrior, it has been too long since we have spoken.

I lowered my head in reverence, squeezing shut my eyes. No one, not even me, was allowed to gaze upon the Lua Pele. Never appearing in physical form, the Lua Pele's presence made itself known in other ways. "Yes, far too long," I whispered.

Burning claws raked over my skin, reminding me of the power of my host. Power I longed to possess. Welts bloomed across my arms and chest, small reminders of our pact. I shivered against the searing pain.

What information do you seek?

"Queen Tessa is our prisoner, she's yours to play with. I seek to know how to break her, how to force her agreement to crown me king."

A sharp stab of pain jabbed between my ribs. I clenched my fists and steeled myself against agony, gritting out words through clenched teeth. "What angers you? Does this not please you?"

Fool. Queen Tessa is not mine and you do not ask to be king, you take it. I grow weary of waiting for you to accomplish such a small task.

Welts appeared on my legs as searing pain tore through me. Anger welled up but I fought it, knowing I could not attack my host no matter what torture was doled out.

"I don't understand, I left the queen in your lair. I have done everything you advised, yet still I am not king as you have promised."

Hoarse laughter stung my ears. *To control her you must control what she loves. If you are the warrior you believe, stop wasting time. Don't ask for a crown, make yourself king. Don't return here until it is accomplished or I will find another and be*

106

done with you.

"We made a deal. Where is my kingdom?"

A throne waits for you at Seamount. Do not fail. The voice faded and water stilled in the cavern. My arms healed and the burning receded, emptiness and frustration swirled in the pit of my stomach. More questions than answers remained.

Nikko and several bull sharks patrolled outside the cavern entrance, waiting for me. Aggression stirred in their hearts in response to my own dark mood, our spirits united for eternity. Our minds linked and Nikko burst out of darkness to my side. Swinging onto his back, I relinquished all thought of belonging to anything but the cold resolve hardening my heart. No more talking, no more waiting. Time to secure what belonged to me.

CHAPTER 15

MOHO
HUHU LOA

RAGE

Leaning forward over Nikko's sleek body, energy surged through my veins, fed by our shared determination and resolve to dominate, to claim Moku-ola as our own. My fingers flexed in anticipation of breaking Tessa's spirit, the crown within my grasp.

As I approached the hole I'd left her in, warning bells flared in my head, the scent and feel of the area violated with an unfamiliar tang. I shifted weight and rose from Nikko's back, nostrils flaring, inhaling the lingering flavor of cinnamon surrounding the Lua Pele lair. Kupua'd been here, I recognized his scent, but the cinnamon was new, even though some part of my brain recognized its sweetness.

On alert, I swung off Nikko and stormed into the lair, tensed for battle with the scent of my brother so close. I knew he had no power to release Tessa from the Lua Pele's grip, but his presence meant trouble and might interfere with my plans. Growls erupted from my throat as I prowled the tunnel, searching for where he hid in wait. Flinging rocks and inspecting crevices revealed nothing but the decayed bones of former victims.

His scent grew fainter the deeper into the tunnel I searched, until no trace of my brother could be detected. He hadn't come inside, or at least not very far. Why would he leave without searching for Tessa, had his fear been greater than his love? My chest puffed, not many had my courage, and none I knew would enter this place, my brother as weak as the rest. Tension slid from my shoulders as all worry about a potential threat faded. Within these vicious tunnels, my dominance held firm, without challenge.

Anticipation wet my mouth, my desire to defeat Tessa a sweet balm to my senses, like sugar on the tongue. My pace quickened. One more turn and I would behold my conquest, and I reveled in the thought of her broken spirit as mine to claim.

Rounding the corner, I staggered, choking on disbelief. Piles of rope lay heaped on the ground, discarded and useless as their captive no longer remained imprisoned. An all-consuming fire raged through every pore of my being, scorching my skin red with fury. My fists clenched as I crashed to my knees, crying out, "Noooooooo." Even though no ears remained to witness my rage, my voice erupted like a volcano, unable to be restrained.

As the rumble within me subsided, my mind lit with questions. How had she escaped? What did her escape mean for the power of the Lua Pele? Pushing thoughts aside I thundered to my feet, embers of rage flaming once again to the surface, unwilling to be quenched. She would suffer for this, when I finished with her and her kingdom there would be no question who held dominance over the ocean.

I swerved and jetted out the tunnel, summoning Nikko and other sharks nearby, gathering them to me and whipping them into a frenzy with thoughts of death and vengeance. Nothing would stop me this time, and there would be no mercy, not for Tessa, or her friends. Only one Kingdom could rule under the sea and with or without her, I would be king and my reign was about to be established.

Catching Nikko by the fin, I glided onto his back, wrapping my arms and legs around his torso, reveling in the familiar feel of sandpaper scraping along my skin. Lethal calmness replaced my rage as I settled in for the trek back to the waters of my youth, back to Moku-ola, where revenge would be mine at any cost.

CHAPTER 16

TESSA

PU

TOGETHER

A full moon cast shimmering light across our path as we searched for a soft place to rest on our return to Moku-ola. Kupua had located a small, sheltered, isolated island where we could catch our breath before finishing our long journey home and now we wandered its ground for the best place to set up camp.

Weighing five hundred pounds each, my legs struggled with each grueling step on dry land, exhaustion dragging at me like an anvil encircling my neck. Kupua, on the other hand, looked as if he could run a marathon, jogging ahead and scouting the area, bouncing from foot to foot. Grumbling, I scanned the landscape.

A soft patch of grass around a bend in the trail called my name and I plopped on my back with a thud, staring at the star filled sky. My muscles groaned with pleasure at being awarded sweet rest and I sighed, relieved to be motionless. Cool blades tickled my skin as I wiggled to get comfortable. Soft ground formed a cradle of comfort around my body, easing my weary bones.

I gazed into the night and watched a star tumble from the sky, its light trailing out of existence. Kupua jogged over to join me. I glanced over at him and whispered, "Quick, make a wish."

His dimples puckered as he smiled at me. "No need to wish, I've already been given the desire of my heart. There is nothing more I need."

My heart stirred as I rolled onto my side and propped my head on my hand to examine him closer. His arms rested on his knees and his head tilted forward as he focused on his hands. His hair spilled over his face, concealing his expression. My heart swelled and blood hummed, and it took every ounce of control for me not to reach out and push back his hair and declare my affection. Memories of the Lua Pele lair flashed in my mind, infusing me with a boldness born from experiencing the fragility of life. Every moment was a precious gift to be treasured and not wasted. Rubbing a sweaty palm across the grass, I swallowed.

"I love you, Kupua."

He lifted his head and his eyes lit. Grasping my hand, he gently pressed his lips to my fingers, shooting a tingling sensation across my skin. "And I love you, Ipo. More than my very life."

I sucked in air. How could I possibly express the depth of what I felt? I lifted my hand to his face and caressed his cheek, tracing the angles of his jaw. "You are a man of honor who loves and cares for everyone above himself. I've never felt such respect, such connection, such love, for anyone else living on earth. I have no doubt the Creator has chosen us to be together. Would you be my king, rule Moku-ola by my side for both our lifetimes?"

He shifted his weight and captured my face with his hands, light shining in his eyes. "Tessa, there's nothing I desire more than to be your partner and king. But, what happened to waiting? To giving yourself time to adjust?"

"I have adjusted. While I wallowed in the filth of that Lua Pele hole, I realized we don't know how much time we have. There are no guarantees, and it terrified me to think I could die without ever having declared my decision to our people, never acknowledging my love for you. I refuse to put this off any longer."

Expressions shifted in his face as he considered my response, mulling over my words. "I understand, but this decision is not to be rushed. You must be sure. There can be no doubts."

"Kupua, I have thought long and hard on this decision and know it is right with more certainty than I know my own name. It is time. Be my king."

He leaned in and kissed me, lips soft and gentle, cupping my face with his hand. He paused and searched my eyes, his voice a whisper. "I am honored by your choice. I accept and pledge my loyalty and protection to you, my queen, my Ipo."

Joy burst from my heart and I felt like dancing but instead I rolled onto my back and nestled against his chest, his arms wrapped around me. Together we surveyed the night sky, peace sinking into our bones in the still of the evening. Stars sparkled above and a slight breeze tickled our skin causing Kupua to tighten his grip on me, his warmth a cocoon of comfort. Soon, all of Moku-ola would know my decision and finally we'd put this issue of crowning a king behind us. Maybe Moho would finally get the message and abandon his battle to be king. One could hope.

A squawk sliced through the silence. A familiar blur of wings and feathers swooped past us and landed a few feet away, flapping, squawking and dispatching feathers in all directions.

"Maxie, what are you doing here?"

She flexed her wings a few times before waddling closer, picking fluff from her feathers with her beak and dispersing puffs into the wind, while she informed me of her mission. Kupua raised an eyebrow at me.

I stroked her neck, smoothing ruffled feathers. She preened under my attention, craning her neck and squawking. She'd flown a long way to deliver her message.

"Kele and Akalei ordered Maxie to search for us, make sure we didn't need them to come rescue us again." I stifled a giggle, covering my mouth with my hand as images of Akalei attempting to calm Kele flickered through Maxie's thoughts. Poor guy, he really didn't like conflict.

Kupua let out a chuckle. "Always playing the hero, our Kele. Have Maxie inform them both we do just fine on our own. No worries."

Maxie squawked, snapping her beak in Kupua's direction.

Evidently she didn't appreciate his lack of concern. She flapped her wings a few more times just to be dramatic, before lifting off, sailing into the night, taking our message home. I leaned back on the grass, yawning. "Give Kele a break, he just worries for our safety."

"He worries too much. But you're right, we couldn't find a more loyal friend." The affection in his voice belied his words. Kele and Akalei held special places in both our hearts. I missed them. I missed Rachel. Thinking about her gave me an idea.

"Are you game for another stop on our way home?"

He shot me a questioning look.

I rolled my eyes. "If we don't tell Rachel our news and she finds out some other way, I'll never hear the end of it. We need to inform her in person I'm going to announce you king before we tell anyone else. Unless of course you'd like to explain to her why she wasn't the first to be notified."

He threw his head back and laughed. "Good point. No, I do not want to face your sister's wrath, or Mike's. We'll make time for a visit. Now, Tessa, get some rest. I'll stay awake and keep watch for a while, just in case Moho decides to make an appearance."

CHAPTER 17

NUHOU

NEWS

We poised ourselves on Rachel's doorstep, hair dripping, sand trailing us up her porch steps and puddles collecting at our feet. Driftwood carved with the word *welcome* dangled above her door, a gift from Kupua. Seashell wind chimes tinkled softly, reminding me of lazy days spent lounging in the sun. I leaned in and rang the doorbell, tapping my foot nervously and jiggling a loose plank below. Kupua clasped my hand and squeezed, calming my nerves and sending warmth oozing across my skin. Inhaling, I sighed at the smell of gardenia and plumeria ever present on the island. Home.

When Rachel finally cracked the door, I launched myself into her arms, hugging tight before I noticed she'd put on some extra weight. She pulled back and covered her stomach with both hands, glowing as she smiled. Realization slowly dawned as my hand covered hers, excitement igniting.

"Really?"

Mike stepped behind her and wrapped his thick arms around her waist, a huge grin bursting from his face. "Yes, Kika, we're expecting!"

My heart swelled, hardly able to contain my excitement, a new family member to love. "This is so awesome! I'm going to be an auntie! How far along are you? Is it a boy or girl?"

Rachel beamed. "About 16 weeks. We don't know yet if it's a boy or girl and don't care, as long as the baby's healthy."

Kupua hugged Rachel. "We must celebrate."

Mike rolled his eyes. "Are you kidding, we've done nothing but celebrate since getting the news. I'm worn out man."

Rachel waved her hand at him. "Don't listen to him, he's the worst of everyone, walking around like a goofy kid since he found out. He already started arranging the baby's room." She paused and took my hands in hers. "But we do need to celebrate your visit. Mike, go call Hiiaka and Puna and have them come over for a barbeque right away."

My stomach clenched, I hadn't seen the former queen of Moku-ola in several months and wondered what she thought of my reign so far, it hadn't exactly been problem free. I loved her dearly, which only increased my desire to live up to her expectations, show her I would not disappoint.

Rachel turned her steely gaze on me. "What brings you here, is everything alright?"

"You mean beside the usual…Moho trying to take over the kingdom, the flute still out there, fish dying, monster shark…blah,

blah, blah…yeah, everything's great."

She patted my arm. "Come in sis, sounds like you could use some rest and a good meal." I grinned, that was my sister's answer to all life's worries: rest and food. Stepping across the threshold, a sense of peace settled over me. All would be well with the world as long as Rachel waited to welcome me home.

Mike and Rachel's home smelled of fresh fruit mixed with baked bread. In true Hawaiian tradition, shoes lined the door announcing the guests within. Yellow walls with windows spanning ceiling to floor kept the atmosphere bright and cheery. Fresh flowers adorned a green wooden table in the corner. Every muscle relaxed as I absorbed the comfort of home.

Rachel kicked into high gear and hustled into the kitchen, yanking food out of the refrigerator and tossing it onto the tile countertop. Ribs, sauce, pineapple, breadfruit, taro chips all in piles, ready for Rachel's magic touch. I perched at the counter and poured myself a glass of lemonade, relaxing into the normalcy of watching my sister cook. Kupua ducked into the backyard to help Mike with preparations, leaving Rachel and I alone.

Rachel looked the same, yet changed. She glowed with happiness and new purpose. I rested my elbows on the counter and sipped my drink. She bustled from sink to counter, preparing food, reminding me of days long past when I'd been a lost little girl who needed my big sister's care. "I've missed you sis."

She froze, her eyes catching mine, glossy with tears. "Me too. It's been a little scary finding out about the baby and not having

118

you to talk to. Mike's great, but sometimes a girl needs her sister."

Setting my drink down, I scooted around the corner and pulled her into a hug. "I know. I'm here now." I held on tight, relishing how her hair smelled of soap and lavender, just like mom.

She straightened and wiped her eyes on her arm. "Times like this I really miss mom. She always knew how to make us feel safe, and I sure could use some advice about this whole pregnancy thing. I don't think I can do it alone."

"You're going to make a great mom, and you won't be alone. We'll all help. I've never had a baby, but I know you…you took care of me, remember." I stroked her hair, allowing strands to linger between my fingers.

She nodded, pulling back and returning to her food preparations, taking deep breaths with an effort to control her emotions. "Thanks, sis. I needed that."

Mike stuck his head in the window from the back of the house. "Barbeque's ready and Puna's on his way over."

I handed him the plate of ribs, nicely seasoned with Rachel's secret recipe. He hesitated, covering my hands with his own. "It's good you're here, Tessa. She needs to see you, to stay close."

"I know." Tears threatened to spill. I needed her too, more than I'd realized.

Hiiaka maneuvered around Mike and spread her arms. "Tessa, it's so wonderful to see you!" Her hug wrapped me in acceptance and warmth, a mother's hug, one meant to encourage and protect. All doubts stripped away as she whispered into my ear.

"You make such a noble queen, risking your life for others. I am so proud of you."

Kupua must have filled her in on what had happened. Something inside me broke at her kindness and I sobbed into her shoulder, my body releasing pent-up wounds. "It's so hard to fight him. I want so much to bring him back to you but he just won't listen."

She stroked my back. "It's not your job to save Moho, Tessa, just to forgive him and love him. I'm sorry he's caused you so much pain." Her voice soothed, but didn't stop me from wanting to do more, wanting to return her son to her.

Mike popped in the window again. "Hey everyone, food's ready. Get out here and eat."

We all sat at the picnic table in the backyard. Birds of paradise formed a border around Rachel's small grassy yard where gardenias bloomed, filling the air with their bouquet. I leaned against Kupua sitting next to me and blissed out. I loved Moku-ola, but this was home too, and being surrounded by family strengthened me.

Hiiaka rose and lifted her glass towards us. "A word of thanks to our Creator for keeping you safe." She turned and inclined her head to Rachel. "And for new additions to our family."

I stood as well, tugging Kupua with me. "We have an announcement to add to the list of celebrations. It's time to crown Kupua my king. I've made my decision and he has agreed. We plan to make the declaration official once we return to the city."

"About time." Rachel chimed, kissing me on the cheek.

"Welcome to the family, Kupua."

Everyone erupted in conversation. Hiiaka left her seat to embrace us, face beaming. "Thank you for coming to share this news with us, I couldn't be happier. Moku-ola is fortunate to have you both."

Mike, somewhat reluctantly held out his hand to Kupua. "If Tessa thinks you're okay, you must not be too bad. Just keep her safe, okay. I don't want to have to make a scene."

Kupua clutched his hand and held it for a moment. "I would give my life to keep her from harm." Mike nodded his head in agreement.

I glanced over at Puna who hadn't budged from his seat and frowned at me when I caught his eye. "Walk with me, Tessa."

It wasn't a question, so I trudged after him to the front of the house and along a sidewalk. He towered over me, a massive hulk of over-protective Hawaiian male. He wore a loose fitting t-shirt with the words "Here today, gone to Maui," which on anyone else might have been funny, but on him seemed kinda scary. Around his neck hung a strand of koa seeds. Several awkward moments passed before he spoke.

"What brings you to this decision?"

"I love him, Puna. He's a good man, full of compassion, courage, committed to serving. He makes me stronger, and when I'm with him, there is no fear, only love. I can't imagine sharing my life, my crown, with anyone else."

He let out a gruff, "Hmmmff," then silence again.

I whirled on him, hands on hips. "What? Why aren't you happy for me?"

He leaned in to face me eye to eye. "There is only one you, Tessa. You are like a daughter to me. When you and your sister came to this island, still grieving the loss of your parents, you became my family. I feel responsible for you. Nothing is more important than family. When the other kids called you haloe, it was me protecting you, defending you. I watched how you bore their insults but never struck back, always forgave. I ask myself, who is this Kupua to deserve such a treasure? You are in love now, but in 20 or 30 years, will your heart still be safe with him?"

I seized his hand in mine. "Puna, do you see how he treats his mother? How he has dealt with his brother's attacks? This is a man chosen by God to rule. This is a man who already has my heart, and there is no turning back for me. Please Puna, I want you to trust me, trust him, and be happy for us both."

His shoulders slumped as the grimace on his face transformed to a smile. Finally. "Okay, my little kika. If your mind is made up, I guess I will give you my blessing." He squinted at me and shook his finger. "But, if he gets out of line or doesn't treat you like the queen you are, he'll have to answer to me, got it?"

I hugged him. "Got it. Thank you."

He rubbed his stomach. "Let's go back and eat now. All this talking is making me hungry."

When we returned to the picnic table, Puna marched up to Kupua and wrapped him into a bear hug, squeezing with all his might. Kupua coughed and patted Puna's back. "Great to see you too Puna. Uh, can you relax a little, you're crushing me."

Puna released him and stepped back. "I officially welcome you as family. Make sure you keep Tessa happy – I don't want to have to hurt you."

Kupua bowed with a sweep of his arm. "I will do my best not to disappoint."

I plopped onto the bench and grabbed a hand full of taro chips. "Great, now let's eat."

Later, Kupua informed me Puna had told him, "Hurt her and I will hunt you down fish boy." Still…progress.

CHAPTER 18

HO'IHO'I

RETURN

Moku-ola sparkled like a gem before me, a welcome sight nourishing my soul. Ocean swirled above my head as brightly colored fish glided across the expansive ceiling shielding the city from water suspended above. Sweet, salty air blew in through lava tunnels and homes below glowed, spilling soft light across pathways lined with polished abalone shells. Children played near a tide pool, splashing water and laughing, their voices drifting up to me, reminding me how many depended upon my decisions. I rubbed my arms, chilled by the enormity of keeping so many safe.

Kupua called me to the table where Akalei and Kele had joined us for an update on news. "Tessa, come eat something." He flashed a quick smile and winked to hide the concern glistening in his eyes.

I plucked a seaweed wrap off his plate, shaking it at him. "I've missed being home. But we can't stay, we've got to find the flute before Henry uses it to wreak more damage. I won't have any more friends hurt."

Akalei bobbed her head in agreement. "We're with you Tessa, but how do we find him? He could be anywhere."

Kele reached for a bowl of fresh pineapple. "Dat guy is brutal, make me fo' huhu, mad."

Nestling into a floor pillow I thought about the dilemma. "I have no idea how to find him, but he can't be far. Moho's probably in the area now that we've recovered Eka and Mimi and wherever Moho is, Henry's sure to be close. Hey, how's Eka adjusting to being home?"

Akalei leaned forward. "She's okay, her mother's taking care of her. The only thing she'll talk about is that art show you promised her."

A pang of guilt stung my heart and I rubbed my temples. "I totally forgot. Akalei, would you arrange the show? I don't want to let her down. See if she has enough to display something in two weeks." I cast a glance over at Kupua. "Maybe Kupua could show off some of his carvings? What do you think?"

Kupua frowned at me. "Not a fan of the idea."

I waved my hands at him. "Come on, be a good sport. Your work is beautiful and our people would love for you to share it with them. Akalei, your thoughts?"

"I'm on it. I'll make it a fun day for everyone." She shifted toward Kele. "You can help me decorate the city and set up the platform over the sacred pool, okay?"

"I all ackshaun for my wahine, yeah?"

She kissed his cheek. "Yeah, all action sweetie."

"Great, at least one thing is settled. Now, if only we had ideas about how to find the flute…anyone?" I raised one hand in question while the other snatched the last chunk of pineapple off Kupua's plate.

Kupua reached for another plate of fruit. "My guess is it's close, somewhere near the islands. I don't think Henry would hide it far from home, he's not stupid."

"You're probably right. But that still leaves a pretty big area to search. There must be some way to narrow our options."

Kupua cocked his head at me. I paused, worried about the glint in his eye and sensing he planned on changing the subject. "We should tell our friends our big news."

My cheeks flushed. Akalei squirmed. "What news? Tessa, you know I don't like it when you keep secrets from me."

I laughed. "I'll tell you but you have to promise not to over-react."

She squinted her eyes at me but kept silent. Kele grunted. "Good luck wit dat."

I inhaled. "I made a decision. I asked Kupua to be my king and he agreed."

"About time. Dis great news," Kele whooped.

Akalei's eyes sparkled with excitement. "Tessa, this is big. We have to plan the ceremony, and the wedding! There's so much to do! How much time do we have?"

I raised my hands. "Whoa, we're not planning anything until we get the flute and stop fish from dying. We also have to figure out what to do with Donnie. When everyone is safe, then we can start planning. Right now, we have to focus."

I needed to check on Donnie. He'd been in a coma state, hidden in a chasm under the care of Sid and his eel friends. I worried our time might be running out, that Donnie's health might not survive being suspended for too long.

Akalei looked like a deflated balloon as she slouched, arms against the table. "Fine. I'll wait, but you have to promise to let me help. Weddings are my specialty."

Kupua cleared his throat. "We need to get back on track people. Henry and Moho are out there preparing their next move, maybe even making it right now. We can't afford to get distracted. As much as I'm looking forward to making a commitment to Tessa, she's right. We have to protect our ocean and our city first."

Spoken like a true king. He wrapped his arm around my shoulder and I leaned against his chest. Once again our hearts and souls hung in perfect alignment and it soothed my nerves knowing we stood together, united.

"So, if you had a magic flute, where would you hide it?"

Kele scratched his chin. "On da surface, round shark bait, someplace close."

I gave Kele a glare. "You have to stop referring to mainlanders as shark bait, it's not nice. Besides, I used to be one of them and my sister still lives on dry land."

He shrugged. "Eh, jus jokin…no gef me grief, das how da bruddahs talk Tessa."

I turned my back on him. "So…let's say we narrow it to somewhere on Maui. Hello, still a big area, where do we start?" I stifled a yawn, the day catching up with me.

Akalei stood and stretched. "Maybe we should all sleep on it. A little rest always clears the head." She set her gaze on me. "You look worn out, Tessa. If you don't go to bed you're gonna fall asleep in your plate."

I rubbed my forehead. We were all exhausted from the journey home from Catalina. I got to my feet. "Okay, sleep couldn't hurt." I looked at Kupua who still sat, arms on the table, circles under his eyes. "You need rest too Kupua, what do you say?"

"I'll go to bed soon. You go ahead, I need some time alone to think."

Reluctantly, I trudged to my room, ready for a good night's sleep in my own bed. I collapsed on my pillows, snuggling under the blankets and fell asleep to the sound of water trickling through the moat surrounding me.

I lay beneath a waterfall, gazing through the cascading water over a pool below. White light hovered on the other side of the falling water, catching my attention, drawing it toward something. The light pulsed, rose above me, as if pointing to a cave hidden in the cliff over my head. A booming voice announced, "Here, Tessa. What you seek is hidden here."

Waking with a snap, I scrambled out of bed and jogged to

Kupua's room, then pounded on his door. He opened it, hair tousled and circles still under his eyes, letting me know he hadn't been asleep for long. He rubbed his head, yawning. "What's wrong?"

I hopped from foot to foot, feeling a chill from the drafty hallway. "I know where Henry's hiding the flute."

He cocked an eyebrow at me. "Really? How?"

I slid past him and plopped on his couch, curling myself around one of his throw pillows. My eyes scanned the carved wooden sculptures hanging from his ceiling. He'd added a new one, or rather a school of new ones. Several barracuda hung in a bunch, faces fierce and protective. I pointed. "Love the new additions."

His eyes followed mine. "Thanks. Carving helps me relax. I tried to do them justice."

"You captured them perfectly. Would you please let Akalei put some of your carvings in the art show? I'm sure everyone would enjoy seeing them."

He gave me a sly smile. "Are you avoiding my question?"

I let out a sigh. "Maybe…I had a dream." He eased down next to me, still and focused, every muscle taught.

"This might sound crazy but the Anela spoke to me in my dream, revealing where Henry's hiding the flute."

"How do you know it was the Anela?"

"I have no doubt it was them, their voices are so distinct, not something one forgets."

Kupua squeezed my hand. "I believe you. So, where is he hiding the flute?"

I swallowed. "On Maui, in a cave over Ohe'o Gulch (Oh-Hey-O), the seven sacred pools. Will you come with me to retrieve it?"

He leaned in, gently pressing his lips against mine. His arm wrapped around me, drawing me closer. His lips warm and soft, drowning out the world as a fire lit my soul, burning against my chest. His love overwhelmed me, pouring into my veins like warm chocolate. Our love a strong foundation, built on trust and friendship. He pulled back and stroked my face with his thumb. "I'll always be with you, wherever you go, whatever you face, my place is beside you."

Our foreheads rested against each other as I absorbed his words and warmth tingled from my stomach to my throat, my love for him overflowing. I wanted the moment to last forever, our problems to vanish, but the thick fog of responsibility hovered, ever present.

"You know we must go alone. It'll be hard enough to sneak up on Henry with the two of us...and I don't want anyone else at risk. We can't tell anyone where we're going."

"They'll understand. Well, maybe not Kele but he'll get over it." He stood, tugging me with him. "No reason to delay, let's leave now, before everyone's awake."

I ran my hands through my tangled hair. "Okay. Would you mind braiding my hair first?"

He swiveled his body behind mine and pulled my hair back with his hands, gently separating the strands into three sections.

"Your hair is so beautiful, like silk."

Holding still, I allowed the warmth of his body to press against my back, breathing in his scent, as fresh as the ocean. As he carefully braided my hair I imagined him as my king, forever by my side. In my heart, I'd already chosen him. Or rather, my Creator had chosen him for me. A calm certainty fortified me as he finished and kissed the top of my head. I twisted into his arms and clung tightly against his chest. "Promise me you won't take any unnecessary risks."

He chuckled. "Weren't you the one who said we couldn't make those kind of promises? After all, as my queen I'm sworn to protect you above all others."

"Then keep yourself safe because I have no desire to rule without you by my side. I love you, Kupua."

Seriousness replaced his smile. "Tessa, we have a long future ahead of us, but if something were to happen, you must rule alone. The people need you. God requires this of you."

I knew he was right, but I couldn't think about how painful such a life would be. "Just make sure I don't have to face that particular challenge, okay?"

"I'll do my best." He touched his forehead to mine and squeezed my arm. "We'd better get going," he whispered, and I felt a twinge of regret at leaving the others.

"Let's leave a note so they know we'll be back, no use in worrying Kele too much."

He scribbled on a piece of paper and stuck the note to his

door, which would be the first place Kele would look for him. Satisfied, we snuck out, hoping my dream would lead us to the flute.

Lizzy waited for us outside the family entrance, her round, brown eyes begging not to be left behind. How did she always know when I was sneaking out? She waddled next to me and rubbed her head against my leg, her soft fur tickling my skin. I glanced at Kupua and shrugged. "I guess one more won't hurt."

He patted her head while I pointed my finger at her. "You can come as long as you do everything I say and no complaining."

She barked and fell in behind us. I prayed she'd be safe. No telling what we might walk into on Maui.

CHAPTER 19

PAKEKAIKO

PARADISE

Rugged, lush, green landscape carpeted Ohe'o Gulch. Tiers of sparkling waterfalls cascading into pools surrounded by volcanic rock climbed the mountainside as far as the eye could see. Behind us, ocean waves roared and crashed against rocks, spilling over into smaller tide pools fed by the swirling mix of ocean tides and waterfalls.

We hiked the trail to the Ohe'o pools, soaking up sun and fragrant air. I followed Kupua, enjoying the sight of his strong form plowing up the hillside with little effort. Although still early, a slight sheen of sweat covered my skin as I worked to keep stride with him. Birds chirped and darted through the ohia trees and ferns along the path. Now and then I'd catch a quick glimpse of a gecko scurrying to hide under a bush. We'd left Lizzy on the beach of the north shore to wait for us. She wasn't exactly made for hiking Maui's rugged countryside.

We stopped for a drink and I eased onto the ground to rest my feet, stretching them out in front of me. A koaʻe ʻula (red-tailed tropical bird) swooped in and landed beside me. Her snowy white body accentuating long narrow tail feathers highlighted with red shafts. She bowed her head and requested to speak. Her formality surprised me, birds usually assumed I'd want to converse, they were a chatty bunch.

I reached out and stroked her velvet feathers, letting her know I'd listen to what she had to say. She called herself Windy. According to Windy, all the birds living near the ocean were upset about fish dying off and wanted to help me put a stop to whatever might be killing them. They'd banded together to form a strategy. She offered to guide us to the cave and explained the plan local birds had devised.

Kupua cleared his throat. "Care to fill me in?"

I pointed to my new friend. "This is Windy. She's going to show us where Henry and the flute are hiding. When we reach the cave, three seagulls, Smudge, Popper and Rex will be waiting to assist inside the cave. Evidently seagulls are well suited for this *type* of work I'm told." Windy bobbed her head for dramatic effect. "The flute's being guarded by a dog and I can't speak with dogs since they're not connected to the sea. That's where the seagulls come in. They plan to deal with the dog, and we're to handle Henry. What do you think?"

He squatted down closer to Windy. "Sounds a bit too easy. Where's Moho?"

Windy let out a squawk and flapped her wings, hopping backwards. I scooted back, smiling at Kupua. "She's not a fan of Moho. He hasn't been seen at the cave but there's rumors among the birds that his sharks guard a back entrance."

Kupua stood. "Sounds like him." He extended his hand to me and I clamped on, jerking myself to my feet, brushing dirt off my legs.

"Do you think Henry will listen? Can his heart be reached by his brother's plea?"

Kupua ran his hand through his hair, shaking out dust from the trail. "We have to try. If we're not ready to give up on Moho, we must have faith Henry can change as well."

My breath caught at the sorrow in his eyes, sorrow for his own lost brother. I laid my hand on his arm. "I won't ever give up on Moho."

He averted his gaze and the resolve in my heart hardened like a rock. What price would I pay to save a soul? How much would I be willing to endure?

Windy lifted off and soared, circling and waiting to lead us forward. I squinted into the sun, admiring her grace as she floated on air currents, much smoother travel than what we faced lumbering over boulders and steep paths. Climbing the rocky trail we followed her up and over several waterfalls, enjoying the cool spray of water as we passed. Finally she perched over a cave next to three seagulls who were squawking, and thrusting beaks at one another like some bird version of toddlers fighting over a favored toy.

I waved my hands at them. "Shhhhooooosh. You're making too much noise."

Smudge, Popper and Rex squawked back and forth about who would take the lead. Wings flapping, they bumped chests, squabbling like bickering children. I raised my hand. "Enough." Seagulls were a noisy bunch and apparently difficult to control. They twirled to face me, each puffing out his chest and nudging the other for a closer position to me. At least they'd stopped squawking.

Kupua shook his head. "Guess taking him by surprise isn't an option."

I shook my finger at the seagulls. "Guess not. You three need to hush and focus. We're here to get the flute, and we work together. No one's in charge, except me, so do your job."

Smudge hopped off the rock and landed on my shoulder, rubbing his neck against mine. I stroked his back. "Okay. Apology accepted. Now, can you three be quiet as we inspect the cave?"

His head bobbed and he spread his wings and flew to join Popper and Rex back above the entrance. I bit my lip, having some serious second thoughts about our plan.

With my back to the rock wall I edged into the cave, using my wrist band to shed light into its depths, revealing nothing but black rock and emptiness as far as I could see. The cave broke off into two tunnels. Smudge glided silently past me, followed by Popper and Rex, immediately choosing the passage on the right.

Kupua and I pressed against the wall of the cave, out of sight of anything exiting the tunnel and held our breath. Before long, deep growling and squawking echoed through the cave. Smudge careened past us and out the entrance, chased by not one, but two huge Rottweilers, snarling and snapping at the birds. Popper and Rex dive-bombed the dogs as they ran, swooping in to peck at their faces before rising out of reach. The group pummeled forward right off the edge of the cliff, both dogs splashing into the pools below, yelping as they paddled to keep their heads above water.

Kupua and I wasted no time, we rushed into the tunnel, our bare feet slipping on the slick rock floor. Bits of fur lay scattered across the ground as we ran, a testament to the skills of our seagull friends. We slid to a stop as the tunnel came to a dead end and looked around. No evidence of a hiding spot anywhere.

I skimmed my hands along the walls, searching for something to indicate a door or passageway, but found nothing. I turned to Kupua. "There must be something here, those dogs weren't guarding this place for nothing."

Smudge swooped in toward us, landing on my shoulder with grace not usually found in a seagull. He hopped to the ground and pecked at the floor next to the wall. Kupua knelt next to him and groped around. A latch clicked and part of the floor rose, spewing a cloud of dust. Smudge squawked and flew off, returning to torment the dogs and wished us well.

Kupua heaved the rock, yanking on the latch and peered into the opening. Reaching in, he plucked out the flute, holding it for me to inspect.

I shuddered. "It can't be that easy. We have to be missing

something?"

He scrambled to his feet. "Let's get out of here and discuss it later."

Sounded like a good plan to me, and we tore out of there. We'd almost cleared the tunnel when Henry lunged in front of us, emerging from the adjacent tunnel and pointing a gun at Kupua. We skidded to a stop and slowly backed up, our focus on the gun he waved. Henry wore shorts and a wrinkled t-shirt, his hair in wild disarray and his bloodshot eyes smoldering with anger, not his usual well-groomed, confident self. He flicked his gun back and forth between us. "Back against the wall, *now*."

Behind Henry I glimpsed a flash of wing, but wasn't sure how Smudge and his friends might react, their thoughts quiet. I steadied myself. "Henry, we've spoken to your brother, it's not too late for you to stop what you're doing with Moho. Sam misses you. Release us and forget you saw us, leave this place and find Sam, he wants you to come home. Whatever Moho's promised you it's a lie. There is no future with him."

He sneered. "Nice try, Tessa. But I don't turn my back on friends."

Kupua edged in front of me, inserting himself between me and the gun. "I know my brother. His only interest is power. He's using you, and will toss you aside once he gets what he's after." Kupua's strong voice echoed off the cave walls.

Henry shifted back and forth on his feet and glowered at Kupua. "We're all interested in power. Why else would you be in this cave?"

I stretched out my hands. "Henry, we don't want the flute for power. We're trying to stop the destruction Moho is causing. Too many lives have already been lost."

He flicked his glance back to Kupua. "I'm gonna need that flute back. Set it on the ground and slide it toward me."

Kupua crouched, hands extended, ready to place the flute on the ground when Smudge dive bombed Henry, knocking the gun from his hand, sending it spinning across the floor and off the edge of the cliff. Kupua and I rushed for the trail leading us back to the ocean. As I looked over my shoulder Henry was huddled in a ball as three flapping seagulls pecked his head. His arms flayed about attempting to knock them away but each time captured only air as they deftly took turns attacking and retreating. I'd never look at seagulls the same way again.

CHAPTER 20

HO'OHOLO

DECISION...DECISION

By the time we reached the ocean, my lungs heaved for air and sweat trickled down my neck dampening the wisps of hair that slipped from my braid. I rested my hands on my knees, catching my breath and fighting the burn in my chest. Kupua wasn't even breathing hard. He flashed a smile as he circled me a few times, his hand tightly grasped around the flute.

"Surely such a short run didn't wipe you out."

I wanted to twist those dimples off his face as I got my breathing under control, not expending the energy to glare at him.

He stopped moving and his voice deepened. "Seriously, we can't stay here, we've gotta keep moving. We have the flute, let's get it somewhere safe. Get in the water and I'll carry you home."

Not going to happen. "I'm fine, I can swim on my own."

He frowned as he handed me the flute to carry while he dove into the sea and transformed into a dolphin. I plunged into the ocean, relishing cool water lapping against my overheated skin. A wave rose in front of me and I dove under it, relieved to be immersed once again in the safety of the sea. Lizzy immediately brushed against me and I wrapped an arm around her, allowing her strength to pull me out to sea, already regretting my defiant refusal for help. I would have to apologize to Kupua later.

Something wasn't quite right. Sounds in the ocean muted; missing an ingredient I couldn't figure out. I tugged on Kupua's fin, slowing him down so I could concentrate to separate out each note of the symphony I'd grown so used to hearing. In the background dolphins clicked and squealed, shrimp crackled, whales…that was it, the missing piece: no whale songs echoed through the depths. Where were they? What had silenced them?

Kupua broadcast loudly for me to keep going, get home and figure it out in safety. Images of Elmo and his mother in danger flickered across my mind. I couldn't go home to safety if they needed me. After all, I'd sworn to protect them, to be their queen. Kupua's acceptance of my decision flowed like warm honey into my heart. Despite his driving need to keep me safe, he supported my choice.

We changed directions and headed toward the whales' normal hangout, diving to the sea floor. Waters darkened and a chill crept over me. Kupua swam alongside and I stroked his slick, smooth skin with my fingers, his nearness offering comfort and protection. Along the bottom we easily scanned our surroundings, visibility providing a clear view, but still no sign of any whales.

Where could they have gone?

Overhead, shadows caught my eye. Sharks gathered, closer to the surface, in larger numbers than normal for this area or time of day, looming silhouettes of danger darkening the sea. We remained near the bottom, safely out of their sight. Kupua switched into an octopus and wrapped his tentacles around my wrists, pulling me behind a rocky outcrop. In a crevice, stuffed into a space much smaller than I imagined he could fit, waited Sid, our ever-present spy.

According to Sid, the whales were safe but had left due to a large number of tiger sharks collecting in the area. With babies at risk, they moved south, out into open water, away from the islands.

Knowing they were safe made the decision to get back to Moku-ola much easier, so Kupua and I headed home, skin tingling with the threat of danger looming over our heads. We dared not risk swimming near the surface, so we crept along the bottom as we ventured home. Afraid for her safety, I sent Lizzy on ahead. If we slowed her pace she would need to break for air while still too close in range of the sharks. Sid agreed to keep an eye on Donnie and the chasm to ensure he stayed secure. Increased sharks gathering in the area could not be a coincidence, Moho certainly lurked somewhere waiting to plague us with more challenges.

When we finally reached the city, Akalei greeted us, excitement shinning in her eyes as she bounced on her toes. "I'm so glad you're finally back. We have so much to do." She hesitated when she saw the confusion on my face. She rolled her eyes. "Tell me you haven't forgotten the art show? I've scheduled it for tomorrow. Eka's been working so hard."

I held out the flute. "Ah…been a little busy here…remember this?"

She sucked in a breath. "You got the flute! But how, where?"

Kupua stepped closer. "Let's go to my room where we can discuss in private, and bring Kele."

Minutes later we congregated in Kupua's room under his sea of carvings dangling from the ceiling. Akalei and I curled on the couch while Kele paced and Kupua leaned against the wall sending waves of calm toward the three of us. He relayed the story of how we'd gotten the flute, ignoring Kele's interruptions exclaiming his dismay that we'd gone without him.

"I no' undastan brah, memba you suppose fo take me wit you fo protection. You one stubborn head. Why you gotta be so pa'akiki?"

Kupua pushed off from the wall and strode over to Kele, stopping just in front of his scrunched face. "Kele, pa'akiki, really? You're really calling us stubborn my friend? Shall I remind you of the time you camped out in front of my door until I agreed to take you above the surface for your 13th birthday? Or, how about the time you refused to speak to me for two weeks when I wouldn't tell you where I hid the pearls I collected?"

I laughed, adding, "Pot, kettle much?"

Kele let out a sigh, threw his hands in the air and plopped onto a nearby chair. Kupua rubbed his hand over Kele's short

143

stubble of hair. "Some things Tessa and I must do on our own. Okay brah?"

Kele crossed his arms in front of his chest and nodded, but kept his lips tightly shut.

Akalei scooted forward on the couch. "Well, now that we got that out of the way, what are we going to do with the flute?"

I rolled it across my palm. "We already tried to play it, which was a total bust. Maybe we should destroy it?" All four of us had tried to play it when we'd first gotten our hands on it, but it hadn't responded to any of our attempts.

"What about Donnie? If we destroy it, what happens to him?"

Akalei had a point. We knew next to nothing about how it brought him here or how it worked. All we knew for sure was we couldn't play it, but Henry and Sam could, and somehow they'd used it to bring Donnie to our ocean and kill a lot of fish. We had squat.

Kupua grumbled. "We can't let it fall into Moho's hands again. As long as it exists he can use it to destroy. Do you really want to take that risk?"

Another valid point. My head threatened to implode. "So…keep out of Moho's reach, check…what else we got?"

Kupua raised an eyebrow at me. "I think we need to talk about the more pressing issue of sharks gathering nearby."

"Right, we've got shark fest happening in our own backyard," I quipped, glancing at Akalei and Kele, feeling a little snarky from all the stress. How many crises could one queen handle anyway?

Kele's head popped up. "Fo'real? You post to tell me dis stuff. Dis is brutal."

Kupua threw his hands out in front of him. "We don't know for sure if it's brutal, but we do need to be cautious, put guards around the city and be on alert."

"What about the art show tomorrow, we can't cancel it, Eka would be devastated," Akelei half asked, half stated.

I straightened. "We aren't cancelling anything. Eka's not the only one needing a break, everyone in Moku-ola could use something positive to focus on. The show is still a go. A little fun will do us all good."

She heaved a sigh and flopped back against the cushion. Kupua smiled at me but his eyes clouded with concern. We finally had the flute, sharks gathered around us, and Moho most certainly was plotting against us…what better time to throw a party?

CHAPTER 21

PA'INA

PARTY

Moku-ola sizzled with energy. Garlands of brightly colored shells strung from house to house throughout the city like tinsel on a Christmas tree. Children danced along the paths to music played by several men gathered by the sacred pool, their soft, sweet melody drifting on the breeze brought in through the tunnels. A hint of mint tinged the air from scented candles floating in tide pools.

Eka's etchings hung from poles scattered around the pool, mounted on polished driftwood and positioned along pathways with notes describing the subjects inspiring her art. I watched from above as she checked on her work and chatted with Akalei, her face a beacon of joy. Despite threats outside our city, happiness prevailed among our people, resilient as spring flowers pushing through the last frost of winter.

I rested my head on Kupua's shoulder, grateful for moments of peace amidst the demands of being queen and wondered once again if anything could pierce the armor of Moho's bitterness. Since he'd first revealed his quest to take Moku-ola for himself, I'd clung to hope he could be reunited with his family and hope didn't waiver, not with his soul in the balance. Kupua squeezed my hand.

"What has you so lost in thought?"

"Racking my brain on how to get through to Moho. I still believe he can be reached, I just don't know how."

"It's been a long time, Tessa, and with every passing year there seems to be less of the brother I once held close and more of the ruthless killer he's transformed into. For now, we need to focus on keeping our promise to protect the ocean and figure out what to do with Donnie and the flute."

"Fortunately for us, I can handle multiple problems at once," I said, laughing at him. "Let's go show Eka some support and check out her art. I'm looking forward to seeing what you've displayed as well." Between Akalei and I, we'd finally convinced him, or maybe bullied him, into including some of his pieces in the show. Either way, I knew everyone would appreciate his work being shared.

His eyes sparkled. "I think you're going to like it, I carved something very special this time."

He followed me down the steps to the sacred pool, clutching my hand the whole way. We hadn't even had time to officially announce my decision to marry and crown him my king. Our news would have to wait, today was Eka's day and some positive attention might lift her spirits. She met us at the bottom step, eyes bright and a huge smile plastered on her face. Her normally wild, curly hair piled on top of her head, pinned in place with an abalone shell carving of a starfish. Her pale pink dress shimmered around her legs, swaying as she moved. Her slim arms still bore faint bruises, which she covered with a sheer scarf tied around her chest. She clasped her hands together, vibrating with excitement.

"Queen Tessa, there's a bidding war over one of my pieces, can you believe it! They want to pay for something I drew. Thank you so much for supporting me. It means the world to me."

I gently nudged her off into a corner to speak more privately. "Eka, no thanks are necessary. You are very talented and it lifts everyone's mood to have a day of fun and appreciation of beautiful art." I narrowed my eyes at her. "How are you really doing?"

She looked down, examining her feet. "I won't lie, I miss Moho, but it's nice to be home and everyone's been so kind to me. Kele even brought me some canvas from the surface."

"Moho hurt you, Eka. Love isn't supposed to hurt."

She looked up, pleading with her eyes. "There's good in him too, he didn't always hurt me. We had fun together, he understood me, watched out for me. He cares about me, I know he does."

"I hope you're right Eka. I want to believe there's hope for him, but I don't get why you defend him and stay with him when he hurts you. Help me understand why you allow him to treat you so poorly."

She twisted her dress between her fingers. "I don't know. I keep hoping he'll be his old self again and I really wanted to show him I wouldn't leave him, that I could be loyal."

I wrapped an arm around her shoulder, hugging her tight. "No matter what happens, never forget how special you are, we love you too."

Her eyes glistened. "I know."

Kupua joined us, gently placing a hand on her shoulder and flashing his dimples. "Eka, would you give us a tour?"

Her face beamed and she grabbed my hand, leading us to her first drawing, a charcoal depiction of reef sharks circling a sunken ship, the details bringing shape and movement to life.

"Wow, Eka, this is incredible. I'd love to have this piece, what is your price." I asked her.

Her eyes sparkled. "For you, nothing. I owe you so much already, it would mean a lot to me if you would accept it as a gift."

I inclined my head, accepting her offer. We moved to the next drawing, this one of three spinner dolphins leaping above the surface. Eka pointed at it. "This is the one being fought over. Can you believe it, a bidding war?!"

"Yes, it's magnificent. I wouldn't be surprised if more people enter the bidding." I'd never seen her so happy.

Kupua tugged on my hand. "Come with me, I have something to show you." He led me to the glass platform over the water of the sacred pool. In the center stood a tall sculpture covered with a tarp. Eka trailed us, bouncing with joy. I reminded myself to tell Akalei to schedule more of these events.

Kupua cleared his throat, grabbed the tarp and yanked, revealing a life size carving of Mimi and Lizzy, leaning against one another, heads together. I gasped and ran my fingers over the sleek, polished wood, tracing the perfect lines capturing their image with such precision and detail. The smell of wood and oil tickled my senses. I turned and flashed him a smile. "This is incredible, I love it, but how did you find time to do this? It must have taken months."

He ducked his head, but I caught the flash of dimples at my remark. "I've been working on it for a while and planned on surprising you, so this event seemed like the perfect opportunity."

My breath caught, I was thrilled at the thought *he'd made it for me*. This beautiful depiction of my friend and her mother, every detail, had been carved for me. One hand covered my mouth and the other reached for Kupua, but before our hands touched, water churned around the platform, rocking it, spraying us with foam and spilling waves onto the glass beneath our feet.

Our joy was suddenly disrupted as Moho rocketed out of the foam and landed a few feet from us on the platform, his body tensed, muscles twitching. A long, razor sharp knife glistened in his hand. His gaze raked across me and landed on Eka who'd gone pale and was slowly edging her way behind me like a frightened kitten. Kupua stepped in front of us both, his hands spread wide in a protective gesture. Moho snarled at his movement but didn't remove his gaze from Eka.

"Traitor." He spit at her.

Eka let out a whimper, so I reached back and grasped her ice-cold hand. She trembled against me.

"Eka belongs here with her family, Moho, as do you. Being

150

with loved ones does not make you a traitor. Trying to kill them, however, is another story." Kupua's strong voice captured Moho's attention.

Moho shifted his stance and focused on Kupua. "You have something of mine and I came to take it back. Where's the flute?"

Kupua plucked the flute from his pocket with a wave of his hand. A breeze blew across my face, chilling me, gone in an instant, leaving me breathless. I watched in horror as Kupua lifted the flute above his head and with both hands, snapped it in half.

A loud crack shuddered through the air. Glass vibrated under our feet, shaking the platform as if the ocean itself roared in approval at the flute's destruction. My feet scrambled for traction on the sleek wet surface but found none causing me to stumble forward. Water surged over the edges of the platform, splashing against my ankles. I stifled a scream as Moho leapt across the distance between us, and in one rolling movement, snatched both Eka and myself, plunging us backwards into the sacred pool, his arm a vise grip around my waist.

Eka screamed out, "Nooooooo," as Kupua's voice boomed, "TESSA!" and he lunged and latched onto my ankle, attempting to rip me from Moho's grip. His fingers bit into my skin, providing welcome connection and hope, but it wasn't enough. My stomach lurched. Water stung my face as we slammed into the water's surface. With force far exceeding my own, Moho broke Kupua's grip and suddenly sharks surrounded us, a barrier blocking Kupua from my sight, their sandpaper skin raking across my arms as I attempted to push them away, fighting to free myself. Eka's arms and legs flailed on the other side of Moho as she attempted to loosen his hold without much success. Water clouded and churned as Moho dragged us out to sea.

I knew from experience fighting Moho's grasp was a waste of energy so I forced my body to go limp, a dead weight for him to haul. Soon enough I'd discover his plan.

My mind whirled. Why had Kupua broken the flute? He knew we didn't know what breaking it might mean for Donnie. Frustration and relief warred within me. At least now I didn't have to make the decision.

Moho dove deeper, his sharks moving in unison, preventing me from seeing past their massive shapes to identify what direction we headed. I relaxed and pushed my thoughts out to Kupua. Reassurance rewarded my efforts; he would follow, and he would always follow me, no matter the danger.

CHAPTER 22

SEAMOUNT

Warm breezes caressed my face, carrying a strange mixture of floral scents and burning ash. Eka and I stood with Moho on a small strip of black sand beneath a sloping mountain. Behind us, the ocean, stretched beyond where the eye could see, a vast wilderness. Overhead, a crisp blue sky was marred only by a plume of smoke rising from the top of the mountain.

"Where are we?" I asked.

Moho released Eka but kept a tight grip on my arm, fingers digging into my skin. I kept my face blank and chin raised, refusing to acknowledge the pain.

"Far from home, Tessa. A place no one will expect, or find, not even Kupua."

Eka twisted around him, trembling, but determination etched on her face. Her hair no longer on top of her head, but wet and plastered around her face, the starfish pin lost. She rubbed her eyes with the back of her hand, smudging makeup under her eyes. "Tori-shima. This island is called Tori-shima. I know because I've been here before. It's a volcano, not far from Japan."

Moho scowled at her. "Quiet. I'll deal with your betrayal later."

Eka winced, flinching away from him.

I'd had enough. Tired of how he spoke to her, I squared off and my voice rose, "She didn't betray you Moho. Why do you always expect the worst of people? She wanted to stay with you, even though you hurt her. She is totally devoted to you, so don't take your failures out on her. Eka's not your problem, I am. And…just for the record, I'm really tired of you kidnapping me…borrrrrinnnnggg."

His face contorted into something resembling a smile. "You don't seem to bore of refusing me the crown, so I decided to build my own kingdom. Welcome to Seamount, Tessa, the *new* seat of power in the ocean." He spread his free arm out wide, indicating the island.

"Seamount? If you have your own kingdom why do you keep pestering me? Just leave us alone and we'll leave you alone."

He snorted and scanned the mountain, I followed his gaze.

A trail wound up the mountainside and I squinted to get a better look at a figure strolling down the trail toward us. Dark hair slicked back, impeccable clothing, cavalier attitude…Henry. He stopped a few feet in front of Moho, slightly bowing. "Everything is ready."

"Good." Moho flicked his hand in my direction. "You are here to bear witness to my crowning and the beginning of a new realm, a rival city to your Moku-ola. And Tessa, there is no such thing as live and let live, as you shall learn."

I froze under his scrutiny, fear paralyzing me for a split second. What would this mean for the people of Moku-ola, for my friends?

Henry yanked my wrists and tied then behind my back. "Sorry, but we don't trust you."

I squirmed, trying to loosen the binding without much luck. "Right back at ya."

He shoved me forward, up the trail, one hand glued to my back. I glanced over my shoulder. Moho bent over Eka, speaking in her ear. Her arms crossed over her chest and her shoulders shook. I bit my lip, hoping she could stay strong under the pressure.

"What's Moho saying to her?"

"None of your business. For some unknown reason, he seems to have an attachment to that little urchin. I don't get it, but to each his own."

Trudging along the trail I appreciated the moderate spring weather, grateful for cool breezes playing with wisps of my loose hair. Henry's breathing labored behind me, guess he wasn't used to all this exercise. Swimming in the ocean had honed my muscles into the strongest I'd ever been. When you swim with sea lions and dolphins you learn agility and endurance, maybe not as much as Kupua, but Henry wouldn't be able to catch me. I quickened the pace.

"Hey, don't think you can out run me. I've got a gun."

Of course he did. "I'm hardly running. And where would I go? It's not like there's a spa waiting at the top of this volcano, right?"

"Funny. Humor's not going to save you, Tessa. You're in over your head this time and nobody's charging in to the rescue."

I thought about the broken flute and wondered what it meant for Henry, for Donnie. Did Henry even know it'd been destroyed? Maybe he should. "This is not the way to get back your flute."

He grunted. "I know it's gone, Tessa. I felt its destruction."

Really? What did he mean by *felt* I wondered. "Kupua broke it. Ended your ability to use it as a weapon against us."

"There are other weapons."

"What do you mean you felt it? Would Donnie feel it?"

"Who's Donnie?"

We rounded a corner and the path grew steeper, causing my thighs to burn with exertion. "That's what I call your friend the megalodon. How will the flute's destruction impact him?" I clenched and opened my fists behind me, dreading his answer.

"You have a pet name for a shark? Wow, you really are weak."

I kept my mouth shut, climbing in silence, waiting.

Henry's breathing quickened with each step. He stopped, catching his breath and jerking back on my wrists, forcing me to stop as well. Sweat trickled down his face. His hair no longer perfectly styled, but in slight disarray. "Since you cared about the shark, I'll tell you what breaking the flute means. It means Kupua sent your pet

156

shark back through the portal. It means the portal to the Lua Pele's world is closed and you'll never see Donnie again."

My knees melted to jello and I crumpled to the ground as joy and sadness battled within me. Closing a portal to the Lua Pele's world had to be a good thing. It meant nothing else could come through to harm us. But, the thought of Donnie lost in oblivion crushed me. Not like we were best friends or anything, but I'd felt responsible for him.

Henry lifted me to my feet, laughing. "How can you even be queen? You're nothing but an emotional, weak, little girl."

His words stung. Even though I knew they were lies, the weight of my own doubts and insecurities laced his words like poison.

As we crested the top of the volcano, Moho and Eka caught up with us, holding hands. Eka kept her gaze on her feet, refusing to glance in my direction. My heart tightened, wishing I could spare her any further pain, but it didn't seem likely. She loved Moho and her love might prove to be her destruction. I hoped not, but it was in the Creator's hands.

We stared into the caldera of an active volcano. Black and grey gravel and rocks scattered among the barren landscape, devoid of plants or any life I could see. Steam rose from vents within its slopes, creating an eerie backdrop to spouting burning ash, which stung my nose. The ground pulsed with despair, wringing hope from my heart. Nothing could survive in this desolate place. Dark clouds gathered overhead and a distant rumbling threatened an impending storm.

Henry positioned me between two boulders, cutting my wrists free of the bindings and keeping his eyes on Moho.

Moho's voice growled. "Tessa, you rule a kingdom built under a dead volcano. Experience the magnificence of communing in partnership with a living one. Behold the glory of Seamount."

Before I could think of a response earth gave way around me and I sunk into the ground. Gravel swallowed me inch by inch, tickling across my skin. Panic rose and I latched onto a boulder, gripping for my life. Henry pushed me off, smirking. "Don't fight it, Tessa. You're going down."

My heart thudded inside my chest, terror threatening to choke me as my throat constricted. Calm, I had to stay calm. I forced air into my lungs, shoving panic out with each breath. I reached out for Kupua, felt his fear for me, his urgent need to reach my location. I shut down the connection. He couldn't help me right now and I saw no reason to cause him further pain. My torso almost completely submerged, I steeled myself for what was coming, hoping I'd be able to breathe wherever I was going. Eka screamed and lurched forward, but Moho captured her tiny waist as she cried out my name in grief.

With a whoosh, earth swallowed me whole and dumped me into a room below. I slammed into the floor with a thud, pain shooting up my back. I rolled to my knees, wincing and attempted to get my bearings, thankful I hadn't been buried alive. A glass partition imprisoned me, separating me from the rest of the room. On the other side, a throne carved from whalebone set against a glowing red wall. On each side of the throne were two chairs lined with red velvet. A crevice in front of the throne emitted steam and gas, dispersing as clouds swirling along the ceiling. From deep within the crevice a scream pierced the silence.

CHAPTER 23

MOHO
MO'I

KING

Molten lava thrummed inside the mountain triggering a fiery response humming through my veins. On top of the world, I surveyed a kingdom to cause even Moku-ola to shudder. *My* kingdom. Vast ocean sprawled around my island like a sparkling blue playground filled with life to conquer. Waves crashed against rocky cliffs with fury.

The Lua Pele's voice infected my soul as its whisper raked across my mind. *Remember our deal Moho. The price of your power must be paid in blood and souls sacrificed to me.* I shuddered at the hollowness its words carved from my heart.

A hand tugged on my arm. For a moment emptiness faded, retreating in the face of emotions as unfamiliar to me as a mother's embrace.

"Moho, what's going on?" Eka scrutinized me, her eyes a swirling mixture of worry, hope and trust.

I leaned over and whispered in her ear. "I have an announcement to make."

We perched on the precipice of the caldera, overlooking the vast expanse of my new domain. I straightened, facing Tessa and proclaimed my kingdom, right before imprisoning her in the soul room. Warm satisfaction spread through my chest as I witnessed her struggle against being sucked into her new prison, knowing her efforts were wasted. The volcano would take her as I ordered.

Eka lunged, screaming and I wrapped my arms around her waist as she kicked and punched my arms. Heat rose in my chest. Since when did she care so much about Tessa? Why did her reaction bother me? Whipping her around, I covered her mouth with my hand and stooped so we stood eye to eye. She wiggled and strained against me. "Stop. If you want to be my future queen your loyalty must be decided, now. Make no mistake, you cannot help Tessa, but your future depends on your answer. Where does your loyalty lie?" Something deep within me tensed, waiting for her answer.

She went limp, her body relaxing against mine. She closed her eyes as tears slid down her cheeks and I released my hand from her mouth. She whispered, "You know I love you. But I care about Tessa, too. Why do I have to choose? Can't I care for both of you?"

"Not if you want to remain with me. Tessa and her friends are my enemies. As my future queen, they must be yours as well."

She wiped her cheeks with the back of her hand, sniffling as she nodded her head. An odd twinge pulsed in my heart, catching me off guard. My stomach twisted into knots. Taking her hand, I tamped down emotions, struggling for control. I could not allow emotional turmoil to distract me when I teetered so close to victory.

Henry snorted behind me. "Are we going to stand here all day? I'm hungry."

I shot a glare in his direction and refocused myself. Tramping down the slope, I maintained a tight hold of Eka as she stumbled on the loose gravel. Henry might become a liability if he kept overstepping his position.

A few hundred feet into the caldera, behind several boulders, hid the entrance to my palace. No more slinking around borrowed caves for me. Steam puffed from rocks, clouding the air with a veil of hot mist. Behind the veil lay a corridor, reinforced with bones woven together like a blanket of death. Poised within, a fifteen-foot monitor lizard guarded the entry, mouth slightly open, eying us with suspicion. With a wave of Henry's hand the lizard lumbered aside, allowing us to pass as it swished its tail back and forth in agitation. Henry's abilities appeared unhampered by the loss of the flute. What wasn't he telling me? How did he manage to control this reptile without the flute? I narrowed my eyes at him as I brushed by, causing him to step back as I took the lead.

Eka clung to me as we strode past the monster, digging her nails into my skin. Her fear drew me close, spiking my interest. My mouth watered, the taste of bitter spices sliding across my tongue. Deep in the waters surrounding the volcano, Nikko stirred, growing anxious for a hunt, sensing Eka's fear through our bond. But before I could hunt, I must be crowned.

Moving through the corridor, the Lua Pele's approval strengthened my control over Nikko's desires. Fear added to the power emanating through the volcano, seeping into my spirit. My muscles hummed and stretched as amplified power coursed into my veins.

"What is that stench?" Eka asked.

Henry chuckled behind us. "Don't worry little urchin, you get used to it."

My grasp on Eka tightened. I growled at Henry before inclining my head to Eka. "You're smelling sulfur. It's part of the volcano. Henry's correct, you'll grow used to it, but it's not as strong in our chambers, closer to the water."

She leaned against my arm as we walked. "Where's Tessa? What do you plan to do with her?"

"She's here to witness my crowning. Be happy she's with us, because while she's here she lives. Others won't be so lucky."

She gasped but said nothing more, but I felt tension vibrating through her body. We rounded a corner and arrived at the chamber of souls, the heart of the volcano. "Eka, Tessa is behind a partition, it blocks her from contacting others and it shields her from the heat of the chamber. Can I trust you to be at my side? Or, do you want to join her?"

She examined the ground biting her nails. "I love you Moho and you can trust me. But, promise me you won't hurt her? She's been a good friend to me and doesn't deserve being held captive."

Henry grunted. "Why do you tolerate this Moho? How dare she request such a promise! Send her back to Moku-ola, she's a liability."

Rage flared, heating my very soul. I thrust out my arm and shoved him into the wall. "Back off Henry, you presume too much. Eka is mine and free to make requests. She belongs in my kingdom and I will not have you questioning me, nor will I tolerate you frightening her." I glowered at him. "Do you understand?"

He threw his hands in the air. "Hey, if you want to be tied to the urchin, go for it, but don't blame me when she betrays you again."

"I never betrayed him."

I smiled my approval at Eka, proud she'd spoken in her own defense. Her hair had dried into tight curls around her face, bouncing as she lifted her chin.

"Good." I thrust my shoulder into the door and it grudgingly opened, unused to giving sway to entry. A blast of hot air knocked us back a step or two. I surged through, towing Eka along. Inside, heat mingled with air from the ocean passages shooting off the main room, making it bearable but not comfortable for those not used to high temperatures.

The soul room existed directly over the Lua Pele's primary domain and the gateway to its world. Lua Pele holes might be scattered across the continent, but this place served as home turf, and exuded intense power, making it the ideal place to establish my rule.

My throne waited against the far wall, beckoning me to claim my place. Henry positioned himself in front of the chair to the right of mine, assuming a place of honor. I moved Eka to the chair on my left and faced the steaming, bubbling, chasm in the center of the room. My eyes made contact with Tessa's as she stood observing from behind her prison wall. Her eyes widened as screams rose from below, piercing the air.

Eka's voice wavered. "What is that screaming?"

"Below us, the Lua Pele holds court. Souls who've lost their way and stumbled into its lair are held, imprisoned, waiting to be consumed."

Eka sunk her nails into my arm. "Moho, we have to help them, we can't just do nothing while they suffer. Please Moho."

I peeled her hand from my arm, barely able to tolerate her whining. She'd spent too long with Tessa, and a twinge of doubt about keeping her crept into my thoughts. "Be strong, Eka. There's nothing we can do for those lost. Unless you want to join them, stand back and be quiet."

She shriveled into the corner, covering her ears with her hands.

Tessa pounded on the partition separating us, but her voice couldn't cross the barrier. The Lua Pele ensured my prisoner could hear me, but she could not communicate to anyone from within her cell. My focus returned to the crevice, time for my crowning drew near.

Inside the vent, steam circled, rising, carrying on top of its curls a crown of bones. It rose above my head, washing me in vapors. Sweat trickled down my neck as steam blanketed me, embracing me in its coils. Sulfur burned my senses, searing away all debris from my thoughts, focusing me on my dark host.

A high pitched, crackling voice cried out. *Behold, King Ka Moho Alii, ruler of my realm, conqueror of the seas. Today I crown you King of Seamount, without rival in your fierceness and strength.*

I dropped to one knee and bowed as the crown descended onto my head. It ripped my temple, digging bones into flesh. I clenched my fists waiting for pain to subside before standing and facing my enemy, craving Tessa's misery as she witnessed my victory. Blood trickled in streams down my cheeks. Hunger from sharks circling below the volcano clenched my stomach. Soon I would answer the call and reunite with them, renewed with power.

I locked eyes onto Tessa as a mixture of terror and grief tore across her features. My voice echoed off the rocks. "Now we will find out who truly reigns in the sea."

CHAPTER 24

MOHO
HO'OPA'I

REVENGE

My body hummed with excitement. Every muscle tensed as I torpedoed through the passage and into the sea while Eka slept, safe and secure in her chamber. She'd been exhausted and relieved when I left her, and now my time to truly celebrate had arrived.

Nikko's impatience to hunt pounded like drums in my head. Glowing red walls transformed to darker stone as I drew closer to the ocean and temperatures dropped, cooled by surrounding ocean. The lava tube abruptly ended at a cliff, dumping into the sea. Pressure kept water from rising and flooding the tunnel, nature's own science experiment. Nikko thrashed below, slicing water with his tail.

I leapt, exhaling with pleasure as salty water welcomed me home, caressing my body with its cool embrace. Too long had I been on land parched and dry. Latching onto Nikko's tail, we sped away from the volcano and into open ocean, hungry for blood. Several smaller sharks trailed behind us, hoping to devour Nikko's scraps. A new shark swam among them, a ten-foot mako, I hadn't seen before. Agile and fast, it darted in between the other sharks, keeping its distance from the group. I made a note to myself to get to know this new follower better. Makos claimed to be the fastest sharks alive and made strong allies.

A metallic scent signaled blood in the water. Nikko switched direction and rocketed toward the tantalizing smell of chum. Stupid surface dwellers, chumming waters to attract sharks, they had no idea how delicate hung the balance between predator and prey. Anger flared in my chest. If this was a trap to harm my brothers, there would be no mercy for the murderers.

The new mako darted ahead with a burst of speed, so I urged Nikko to rev up, but also sent caution through our bond, better the mako suffered harm than us. As we approached blood infused waters, warnings exploded in my head. A fishing line, barely visible in cloudy water spread out in front of us as the body of a finless shark floated past, sinking to the bottom, ravaged and bloody. I clenched my fists as rage swelled within me, burning deep in my heart.

Releasing Nikko, I swam to the surface. Silently breaking through waves next to the boat, I scouted the situation. Blood choked out all other scents, an overwhelming invitation for attack. An older man and two younger ones tended lines. They shouted back and forth, oblivious to the presence of their impending doom. I rammed the boat and hurled them off balance before swinging onto the deck and unleashing my fury. One of the younger men pitched forward and I wrapped my hand around his throat, strangling until soft flesh collapsed, his eyes bulging as the other two yelled and swung at me. I launched the man in my grip over the side of the boat, knowing Nikko would devour him. His screams lasted mere seconds before being silenced as his head disappeared below the surface in a cloud of red.

I ducked as the second man swung his fist in my direction. Twisting, I used my foot to kick him over the side to join his friend among the thrashing throng of frenzied sharks. I straightened and focused on the older Japanese man, his face lined from years of hard life on the sea tormenting my sharks. He cowered behind a pile of fishing net and beside a stack of shark fins; testaments to his guilt. Fear poured off his body like a sweet intoxicant. My chest burned, madness eclipsing rational thought as the blood of my brothers assailed my senses and revenge tightened its stranglehold on my soul.

With two steps I reached my prey, snatching his ankle and heaving us overboard, his leg tightly clamped within my grip. He kicked and punched, struggling for his life, but my mind was far beyond feeling anything but the hunger for vengeance. Nikko waited below the boat, pieces of flesh dangling from his teeth. I tossed the man in front of Nikko and with one quick movement, he ripped the man in half, diving with his prize gripped between his jaws. Smaller sharks approached and I released what remained of my prey to their ravenous care. No more sharks would fall to his treachery. Vengeance faded, replaced with the sweet satisfaction of success.

Glancing around, I searched for what had become of the other man. In the distance I spotted the new mako with something clenched in its jaws and did a double take. Was he lugging the human by the shirt? I called for Nikko to investigate this bizarre sight, suspicious something might be wrong with this strange shark. Nikko swooshed past and I latched onto his tail, anxious to figure out why a mako would pull a surface dweller toward shore. An idea nagged at the edge of my awareness: sharks didn't play with their food, they ripped, tore and devoured their prey as efficiently as possible.

Overtaking the mako's speed proved impossible as suspicion melted into certainty about the identity of this shark. Only one person would be foolish enough to save a surface dweller from a swarm of frenzied sharks. Kupua. Nikko and I watched as he released the human into the shallows and whirled, aware of our presence closing in.

We charged, fury propelling us through the water, how dare he intrude here, so close to my newly established kingdom. At the last moment Kupua spun to the side and jetted away, his speed beyond what even a normal mako could achieve. Nikko and I pursued as I roared to my sharks for assistance, I would not lose him again.

Kupua's acceleration as a mako kept him just out of reach, navigating swiftly through twists and turns meant to slow me. Other makos responded to my summons, quickly catching my brother. Two flanked him on either side, boxing him in, diving, spinning, they careened through the sea sending fish fleeing in their wake. A squid, swerving to avoid the mass of sharks spun unsuspecting, straight into Nikko's mouth. Nice.

My makos forced Kupua toward the bottom, nipping at his sides until blood trailed like a bright ribbon in the currents. Nikko and I gained on the group, anticipation coursing through my veins at being so close to finally tasting victory over my brother. How fitting Kupua would be the first conquest in my plan to destroy Moku-ola.

Nikko exploded into the group and I snagged Kupua by the tail, swinging onto his back. He spun, attempting to throw me but I held tight to his dorsal fin. As I leaned over to gouge his eyes he began to vibrate and a bright light momentarily blinded me, loosening my grip. He lurched, flinging me off in a cascade of bubbles. When I opened my eyes I gaped into the black orbs of an orca.

Backpedaling, I desperately searched the water for Nikko, knowing there wouldn't be time to escape if Kupua decided to strike. Before Nikko could reach me, the orca attacked, pining my arm in its razor sharp jaws and towing me away from the scene. Teeth tore into my flesh, ripping deep to the bone, shooting searing pain up my shoulder. Blood clouded the water, filling my mouth with the metallic tinge of my own scent.

Nikko erupted, berserk with bloodlust, pursuing the orca with death foremost in his mind, our souls as one in our desire to destroy.

171

Relentless, I knew he would not give up until he avenged my loss.

Fuzziness blurred my vision, life sustaining blood draining from my wound too quickly to maintain focus. Weakness loosened my muscles as I relinquished control, my arms and legs going limp and my body dragging against the current. My last thoughts drifted to Eka, alone and unprotected with Henry. Would she be safe when I didn't return?

CHAPTER 25

MOHO

PIO

CAPTIVE

A woman's voice whispered in the darkness, and from recesses deep within my mind, I drew nearer to the sound, as if a long lost memory had returned in the flesh.

"How much longer till he wakes?"

"Eh! Move outta da way, I amost done. Dis one wake up soon."

"Kele, how are we going to convince him to tell us where Tessa is? We have to find her."

"Fo'real? Garans my brah, Kupua, will get da information. No worries."

Awareness inched its way through the fog of confusion clouding my thoughts. My mouth caked like dried seaweed and my lips cracked when I attempted to speak. A weight pressed against my arms and legs, restraining my movement. Heat rose within my chest, building like a pressure cooker. They had me tied.

I cleared my throat, rasping, "Release me or you'll regret it."

Kele stood over me, raising an eyebrow at my threat. "Naff awready. Don't be li'dat. Memba, befo time, wen we were brahs?"

I growled. Akalei took two steps back. "I'll go get Kupua now."

Kele nodded and returned my stare, a stupid grin plastered on his face. "Dis should be fun."

I scanned the room, hoping to locate something I could use to escape. Driftwood rails hung from the rock ceiling, layered with green bandages dangling like limp noodles. Three beds pushed against the walls, cleaned and stripped waiting for use, smelling of mint and soap. In the center of the room a large tide pool steamed, emitting swirling fog through the air fused with lavender. They'd brought me to the healing room, deep within the palace, a place far removed from any access to open ocean. I'd been in this room once before, long ago when my father had been injured during a trip to the surface. He'd been struck by a boat and suffered greatly. Surface dwellers were careless and cruel, unaware of the harm they caused so many in the ocean.

Moments later, Kupua arrived, dogged by that smelly sea lion Tessa loved so much. Kupua's eyes shimmered with anger. His hand held his side and he walked slightly crouched, wincing in pain. "Hello brother, welcome home to Moku-ola."

I clenched my fists.

174

He tilted his head. "What, nothing to say?" He stepped closer and bent over, his face so close I could smell his fear, fear for his queen who remained captive within my kingdom and beyond his reach. Confidence bolstered me. I still had something he wanted; someone he cared about.

"At least I'm not screaming. More than I can say for your queen."

Kele gasped next to him, but Kupua straightened, a feral glint flashed across his expression before vanishing, replaced by a calm mask of resolve. "We'll see."

With my arms and legs still bound with seaweed rope, Kupua and Kele lifted me off the bed and carried me to the steaming, deep, tide pool. My arm throbbed with pain despite the thick wrap of medicine Kele had applied. I gritted my teeth as they lowered me into the soothing, warm water and despite being lashed to a post about 10 feet under, the throbbing in my arm subsided. Medicinal scents of lavender, horsetail and garlic assailed my senses. I hadn't been in the healing pool before, its calming effect oozed into my muscles, erasing the stress of my injury and making me a bit drowsy even though I fought the effects, determined to remain alert in the presence of my enemies. Unable to move my arms or legs, I waited, curious what they had planned.

An octopus slid into the pool and wrapped itself around my ankle, suction cups pulsating against my skin. I kicked my leg attempting to dislodge the thing, but it held tight like glue against my skin; a repulsive creature, lacking the raw aggressive courage of a true predator. Even more pathetic, a small seahorse followed, attaching to my other foot, curling its tail around my toe. Were they going to hug me to death? Neither creature spoke, appearing to be absorbed in their own internal conversations. My hands wrenched against the rope, attempting to loosen its grip to no avail. Even wiggling my toes made no progress in dislodging the seahorse.

My eyes widened as my mother eased into the pool. I ducked my head, observing from the corner of my eye as she floated to the bottom, sitting across from me, face to face, her hair coiled in a braid atop her head. She wore a dark green dress, tied at the waist, which ballooned around her as she settled against a mossy wall. Beautiful as always, now she carried a weariness about her and small lines marked her face with the passage of time. A second, younger woman joined her, holding a hand in front of her swollen belly. She had to be Rachel, she closely resembled her sister. Her bright eyes sought my gaze, determination and resolve hardening her expression. I closed my eyes, not wanting to make contact with either of them, but helpless to avoid their scrutiny.

A hand gently pressed against my bandaged arm. Even with eyes closed, I recognized my mother's touch, soft and encouraging. My heart ached with a flood of memories, before I clamped it shut, refusing to submit to weaker emotions. I'd shut her out long ago and had no intention of letting her in now, after so many years apart. Warmth pulsed through her hand into my arm and pain receded, causing me to silently curse my mutinous arm. Tension released its hold on me despite my valiant efforts at defiance and I relaxed against the post behind me, lightly banging my head against the wood in frustration at my body's treachery.

My mother's soft voice weaved its way into my mind as she spoke, sending tendrils of love intruding into my consciousness. "I will always love you Moho. You will never be harmed here in Moku-ola. You are in this pool for healing. Allow us to heal you, my son, both your physical and emotional wounds."

A lump formed in my throat. I would not give in to tears, even as they pushed against the lids of my eyes, longing for release. Too many walls had erected in my heart, too many years spent resisting the draw of family. Pain in my arm lessened, but the hardness in my heart coiled against the onslaught, opening wounds anew, stinging and raw at the remembering, bringing their own fresh pain. Some wounds, once born so long, become too familiar to release.

Another voice crept into my mind; a darker, more familiar voice. *Don't listen to her lies, Moho. She only wants to trick you into revealing where you've hidden Tessa. She doesn't love you, she abandoned you. You are mine.* The Lua Pele claimed my soul, never leaving me alone for long. Now, in my weakened state, the Lua Pele reminded me whom I belonged to and where my allegiance was owed.

I squirmed under the assault, conflict and turmoil boiling within, as part of me longed to believe my mother, to accept her love, while the more rational side remained fully aware of my bargain struck with the Lua Pele; a bargain which could not be

177

undone and live. But, the door to my mother had been long closed. So, with little effort, I slammed it shut again, erecting defenses around my heart with the ease of long practice.

Years ago, after discovering my gift and fighting for control over the sharks, I'd hidden, hoping my mother would reach out to me, find me, comfort me, instruct me on how to deal with such imposing power, hoping she would help me gain skills I so desperately needed to survive. Sharks weren't forgiving by nature and I'd had no preparation for the struggle I found myself in for survival among those powerful beasts. But she never came. Instead, the Lua Pele had offered assistance, during the hour of my greatest need and secured my role as ruler of sharks. In return, I'd promised my loyalty, my devotion.

"Son," my mother's voice broke into my thoughts, "I have always loved you. Your father and I searched for you that day so long ago, we ached to help you but never found your hiding place. I'm so sorry you had to endure so much alone, please forgive us and return to your family. There is no weakness in loving others, only strength."

Her voice tugged my heart forward, bulldozing through my chest, releasing desires I'd long suppressed. But, the Lua Pele exploded in my mind, pressing those emotions back into hidden chambers, locked tight. *Lies! I found you, it was I who helped you and crowned you king. You are mine*!

I opened my eyes and glared into my mother's face. "I am no longer your son. You relinquished that right long ago. You will never see Queen Tessa again."

CHAPTER 26

TESSA

KOKUA

HELP

Sweat coated my back as I longed for cool water rushing against my face and the fresh scent of open ocean. I knotted my damp, stringy hair into a ball on top of my head, fanning my face for any relief from the thick, heavy, stagnant air. My throat burned from screaming, and lack of water didn't help. I'd drained the small pail provided to me by Moho.

Moho, Eka and Henry had left me alone after his crowning, laughing and celebrating Moho's victory as they exited. Who knew how long I might be isolated in this nightmare. No matter how hard I tried, something blocked my ability to call Kupua or any of my friends in the sea. Alone, captive, I determined to secure my own escape but after racking my brain for hours I still had zip for ideas.

As I searched the walls and floor for possible weaknesses,

Eka crept into the chamber, crouching low and glued against the wall, as if afraid to be noticed. She slowly approached the clear partition separating us and held her finger in front of her mouth for quiet.

She pressed her face against the partition and whispered. "Have you seen Henry?"

I shook my head no. Luckily, he'd stayed away. The guy really creeped me out.

Relief washed across Eka's expression and her body relaxed slightly. "Good. Even with Moho around, I don't trust him, and I know he doesn't like me."

Uh, major understatement, but I kept listening, wishing she could hear me.

"Tessa, I'm going to figure out a way to free you from this prison. Moho left to swim with his sharks and I don't know how much time I have, but I'm going to go above and examine how they put you in here to see if there is some way to release you."

I shook my head violently. No way did I want her risking her own safety, not now, not ever and especially not with Henry lurking around somewhere. My fists pounded on the glass but her face hardened and she straightened. This wasn't the Eka I'd first met in Moku-ola, having dinner with her parents. Life's sharp edge had strengthened her resolve.

"I can do this, Tessa. After everything you've done for me, I have to do this." She swiveled and left, hugging the wall back to the door she'd entered. I pressed my body against the glass partition and slumped to the ground, tucking my knees to my chest and wrapping my arms around them. My forehead fell against my knees, as I prayed for Eka's safety. Instead of worrying, I poured energy into praying she would stay free of Henry's notice.

It didn't take long before I heard scraping from the ceiling. "Can you hear me, Tessa?

A small rock fell through, pinging off the wall onto the floor. "Yes. Can you hear my voice?"

"I can! I might be able to send a rope through for you to climb out. Hold on."

I stood, wringing my hands. Maybe this would actually work. I paced back and forth across the room, nerves tingling with anticipation.

My hope deflated when Henry burst into the chamber of souls, wearing a smirk on his face and sauntered in my direction. With a quick pivot my back greeted him, grateful he couldn't hear me and called to Eka. "Eka, don't send anything, Henry showed up. Wait."

More scraping above me and then she responded. "Okay. Let me know when he's gone. I've got a rope ready."

I kept my back to the partition, hoping Henry got the message I wasn't interested in anything he had to say. No such luck.

"And here I thought you'd be happy to see me," he said. "It can't be very entertaining all alone in your cell."

I peered over my shoulder, no use in speaking, he couldn't hear a word I said through the partition.

He slunk closer, and the hunger in his eyes sent chills shivering along my spine. Somehow, this man had lost his soul and whatever had taken its place craved pain and destruction. He leaned against the clear partition and observed me from the corner of his eye. "I don't understand why Moho bothers keeping you alive. Seems to me you're more of a liability, we'd all be better off if you weren't around causing trouble."

I swallowed bile threatening to surge up my throat and wrapped my arms around my stomach. I thought of a snarky reply but he couldn't hear me so I just faced him and glared.

Henry chuckled. "I've got a story to tell you, queen. Since you're not going to be on this earth much longer, I thought I'd let you know just how out matched you are and why you won't hold on to that crown you don't deserve." He shifted position and lowered his voice. "You've heard of Moho's great grandmother, Hazel, the one who became queen of Moku-ola all those years ago after being shipwrecked?"

I nodded, wondering what secret he hoped to reveal.

"Hazel had a younger brother. The family hadn't wanted to risk his health with a long voyage so they left him with relatives, thinking they'd be back after Hazel's marriage. But they never returned and the young orphan grew into a man, inheriting the family titles and estates. He eventually married and had children of his own, including my grandfather."

He paused. "Of course, none of us knew what became of Hazel, never imagined Moku-ola existed. But the family legend of the flute passed down through generations, handed from son to son as a priceless gift of knowledge, finally spoken to me. So I decided to search for it, go on a treasure hunt. It wasn't hard to find information on the shipwreck and money was no barrier, I've got plenty of it.

About two years into my search I finally discovered Hazel's ship. Did you know it was named Two Brothers? Ironic, right? Anyway, I personally made the initial dive to explore the area. Everyone was a bit freaked because an uncommon number of sharks gathered in the area, almost as if they guarded the ship. The moment I uncovered the flute and took possession, I felt its power, knew I could wield that power. Then Moho arrived, riding on the back of his shark, quite impressive. He planned to steal the flute from me, but I'd already claimed my prize and understood its value. Because I possessed the flute, no shark would approach, my own personal shield. We agreed a partnership might benefit us both, and now, here we are, all the ocean ours for the taking. We are Hazel's bloodline. You are an intruder, unworthy to bear a crown upon your head."

Clearly, Henry had issues. Poor Sam. Kupua would be interested to hear he had cousins of a sort. Crazy, power hungry cousins, but you don't get to pick your family. I sighed and crumpled on the hard floor wondering if Henry had more revelations to spring on me.

His eyes became emotionless pools of blackness, tracking my movement. "And now you and your boyfriend have destroyed my flute. Sooner or later, I'll get my revenge for that, Tessa. You can

184

count on it."

I shuddered as he spun and stalked out of the chamber, without looking back.

I called to Eka. "He's gone."

Her voice sounded a bit shaky. "Are you okay? He's kinda intense."

Another understatement. "Yeah, I'm fine. At least now I understand how he fits into Moho's plan. Did you know they were related?"

"No, Moho didn't tell me. He doesn't talk about Henry at all when we're together. I don't think he even likes Henry."

"Huh." Store that piece of intel for use later.

More scraping and thumping rumbled above me, resulting in a few small rocks showering my head through the ceiling. "Hey, be careful, what are you doing anyway?"

"I'm pushing a rope through, get ready."

Oh, I was so ready. Slowly, the rock ceiling separated just enough for a rope to drop through, gravel cascading onto the floor. I covered my head with my hands, waiting for it to stop. Brushing rocks off my shoulders I stepped under the rope, hauling myself off the ground and planting my feet on the wall for leverage.

Concentrating on my climb, I failed to notice Henry coming back into the room until his roar sliced the silence. "What are you doing?" Footsteps stomped. "Well, my chance came sooner than I thought, this should be fun."

Every muscle tensed. Glancing over my shoulder I caught

sight of his back as he rushed out the room. Increasing my pace, I shouted to Eka. "Eka, get out of there, Henry's found out, he's on his way."

"Sorry, Tessa, I'm not leaving you."

Ughhhhh….I had to reach her before Henry. As I approached the top I propelled off with my feet and broke through the ceiling, head first, crashing through gravel. Sunlight blinded me as I hauled myself through, Eka grabbing my arms and yanking me fully onto the barren landscape of the caldera.

A scream escaped my throat as Henry loomed over Eka and lifted her off the ground, one arm circling her waist. She shrieked, kicking and punching him like a tiger caught in a trap.

"Let me go…Moho told you not to touch me!"

Henry smirked, glaring at me. "Moho isn't here is he? And I don't think he'd appreciate you helping the queen escape. Naughty little urchin."

She stilled, fear creeping over her face. I stood, brushing sand and gravel off my arms. No longer blocked by the chamber of souls, Henry was about to learn what being queen meant. I closed my eyes and focused, calling for immediate assistance. Soaring in the clouds, my friends responded in force. A group of pelicans swooped to my aid, thrusting and snapping their bills at Henry's head. He dumped Eka, waving his hands in the air, defending against their onslaught.

I nabbed Eka's arm and scrambled up the side of the caldera, eager to reach water and home. Eka panted as we climbed, her petite

186

frame working twice as hard, her chest heaving with exertion. Once we hit the top, pummeling down the trail took no time at all as we navigated loose rocks and boulders. Soon, Henry's screams were a distant murmur, lost to the breeze.

Eka hesitated at the shore, a dozen emotions flicking across her features. "I'm not sure I can leave Moho," she pleaded. "I love him, Tessa. He needs me. I need him. I promised to stay with him."

Placing a hand on each of her shoulders, I employed my most commanding queen voice. "You cannot remain here with Henry, not now. I won't leave without you so make your decision. Safety in Moku-ola or Henry's wrath?"

She bit her lip, squirming under my gaze, her face turning various shades of red. A few moments passed as she battled with her decision, wringing her hands and jumping from foot to foot. I prayed she'd make the right choice, I really didn't want to deal with Henry or Moho on his own turf. Finally, she whispered, "Okay, I'll return with you for now. But I'm not promising to stay."

"Good enough." I clutched her hand and we fled into the water. Now we just had to make it back without barreling into Moho and his army of razor-sharp teeth.

CHAPTER 27

ALOHA

FAREWELL DONNIE

Back in the cool water of the makai, my spirit soared, as familiar squeals of whale and dolphin hummed like music to my ears. My senses reached out for any friends nearby and a pod of spinner dolphins responded, offering assistance to transport us home quickly.

One stop was necessary before we returned. Henry's comments about Donnie's fate haunted me. I needed to know if he spoke the truth; if Donnie had truly vanished from our world, sucked into some portal back to the depths of an evil Lua Pele world.

Competing emotions rolled through my stomach as part of me hoped he still slept safely below while another part felt relief he would never threaten my ocean again. Nervously biting my lip, I drew closer to the chasm. Eels buzzed with excitement, something had the typically reclusive group roused and talking. We paused before descending, steeling ourselves for what might be waiting in the murky depths. Eels normally kept to themselves, hiding in crevices along the wall, but today they were out and chatting up a storm.

It didn't take long to catch the general theme of the day. Donnie had indeed disappeared. None of the eels understood how or where he had gone, but not one doubted he no longer waited, dormant, in the cavern below. I increased the pace, anxious to see for myself and check in with Sid. Maybe his octopus senses caught something others had missed.

When we originally sealed Donnie into the cavern a gigantic boulder had been moved to block his escape. Now, nothing remained of the boulder but rubble. Something had blown it to bits. I plucked one of the pieces, rolling it across my palm, amazed at its warmth. Normally cold to the touch, this rock emanated heat, but why? What had happened?

Dropping the rock, I motioned Eka to continue pressing ahead toward the cavern, hoping Sid had answers. Sounds muted as we emerged in the cavern's pool and crawled onto the sandy beach. Rocks from the boulder littered the area, more evidence of an explosion. I frantically searched the area for Sid and found no sign of him. Had he been hurt?

Eka settled on the beach while I eased into the dark water refusing to give up on my friend. Using my hands, I explored crevices along the submerged wall, hoping he'd found some safe sanctuary among the many holes peppered in the porous volcanic rock. Sharp edges bit at my fingers, scraping and scratching until they bled. Finally, in one of the deeper cracks, my fingers discovered a rubbery tentacle tucked against the far wall. My heart raced, ecstatic I'd found him.

Clutching several limp tentacles, I gently extracted my octopus from his safe haven. With his lax body cradled in my arms I returned to the open air cavern holding my breath, praying for life to animate his still body once again.

Eka and I sat with our legs in the water and Sid floating between us, gently stroking him and hoping he'd wake. I couldn't find any signs of trauma on his body and felt certain he was only in shock.

"Tessa, can you reach him or try to wake him with a command?" Eka asked.

"I don't know, I've never done anything like that before but it's worth a try." I concentrated, prodding Sid's brain, searching for flickering glimpses of thought and detected a tiny spark of life. "I've got something!" I whispered to Eka, grasping on to hope. With renewed effort I commanded Sid to wake, to respond to my command. For a creature of the sea, my summons exuded great power and authority awarded to me by the Creator. None could refuse me if I commanded, except the sharks, for reasons still unclear. Moho's gift provided them immunity to my call.

Sid's spark grew brighter and his body trembled, slowly waking. His tentacles squirmed, fanning out and curling in tight to his body. Colors streamed across his skin; blue, orange and green and ink clouded the water around him, a natural defense to his vulnerable state.

"Welcome back my friend," I cooed. I glanced at Eka who beamed, brushing back curly hair from her eyes.

"I knew you could do it, Queen Tessa."

I stroked Sid's head. "Now, tell us what happened to you, my friend."

According to Sid, a vibration in the water alerted him to something amiss. Eels retreated deep into their homes, sensing danger as sulfur permeated the area choking out all other scents. Donnie remained in his comatose state, never waking, oblivious to changes around him when a sonic boom blasted through the cave. Sid barely got to cover in time, but didn't escape being knocked unconscious. He still seemed a bit disoriented.

No sign of Donnie anywhere. Henry must have been telling the truth. Donnie had returned to where Henry had summoned him from, gone for good…my only consolation being he likely didn't feel any pain or even awareness at what was happening. I dropped my head and took a moment to say goodbye, a final farewell to a creature I never expected to meet. We might not have been best buddies or anything, but I still felt responsible for the guy. He wasn't just another pawn in Moho's games, he was a living, breathing creature.

Eka placed her hand on my arm. "There's nothing you could have done, Queen Tessa. It's not your fault – it's Henry's for bringing him here in the first place."

I knew she was right, but it didn't ease the ache in my heart.

191

Why did life have to be so complicated? I wiped my eyes and secured Sid in my arms, cradling him against my chest. "Let's get back to Moku-ola. Kupua and the others need to know what happened here."

CHAPTER 28

LOLI

CHANGE

Our footsteps squeaked on the smooth, polished, abalone shell floor of my home in Moku-ola, as we crept into the family sitting room, right outside my bedroom. Soft light emanated from the walls, gently illuminating the empty white couches. No guards, no family, just an eerie silence greeted us.

"Where is everybody?" Eka whispered.

"No clue, wait here," I instructed, as I dashed to my room and gently slid Sid into the moat surrounding my bed where he could rest and recover without being disturbed. He curled himself into a tight ball and snuggled into an empty conch shell, happy and content. I experienced a twinge of envy, wishing I could tuck myself away from the world for a time as well.

Hopping into the bathroom, I peeled off my filthy dress, smudged with dirt, sweat and ash. I changed into a comfortable pair of shorts and a t-shirt. After splashing water on my face and throwing my hair into a fresh ponytail, I paused at my reflection. Nothing much appeared different on the outside, but in the recesses of my stare hung the burden of knowing evil's plan. The Lua Pele wouldn't stop at destroying Moho, it wanted to claim everyone belonging to the Creator. This was war and love was my most powerful weapon. Stakes were high and a shudder passed through me before I straightened my shoulders and hardened my resolve. Declaring myself ready I returned to Eka, more determined than ever to conquer this enemy.

"Let's go find the others, they've gotta be around here somewhere."

Eka traipsed after me into the hall where the smell of breadfruit grilling made my mouth water and my stomach rumble. I winked at her. "Time for dinner." We burst into a run, racing through the halls.

Kupua sensed my approach and intercepted us as we reached the dining room, sweeping me into his arms and spinning in a circle. Burying his face in my neck, inhaling deeply and whispering, "Thank the Creator."

I clung to him, as my courage dissolved and emotions unraveled, a trembling heap of crying queen. He smelled of ocean and soap, a safe place where I felt loved, protected and calm. When he pulled away to look me over, my skin shivered from the loss of his warmth.

"Tessa, are you okay, did he harm you?"

My teeth chattered, emotions thrusting me into a state of

shock. "Well, he didn't exactly roll out the red carpet, but I'm fine…now." Memories of being held captive stirred, clawing at my heart, but I stuffed the thoughts away to deal with later. I had to get it together before facing the others, who I knew were waiting, giving Kupua and I time to connect before descending upon me with their own relief and happiness. One thing I'd learned about being queen was your life no longer belonged to you alone; others had a stake in your well-being.

Kupua dragged me back into a hug. "We were all so worried about you. There is much to tell you."

"Yeah. I've got some news myself."

He raised his eyebrow at me before tugging me into the dining area where my friends waited, keeping a tight hold on my hand, his warmth grounding me with much needed strength.

I glanced over at Akalei, her arms wrapped protectively around Eka who looked like a cat being prepared for a bath, outward expressions of affection not exactly familiar to her. Akalei remained oblivious to her discomfort, but then Akalei assumed everyone needed a hug, one of her many endearing qualities.

Akalei released her hold on Eka and slammed into me. She squeezed tight while simultaneously bouncing like a bunny on steroids, determined to mix my insides like fruit in a blender. "I can't believe you didn't take me with you! I should have been there to help you escape!"

Grabbing her shoulders to stop the vibrating, I steadied myself. "I think you're missing the point of being kidnapped, there's not a lot of choice in who gets to come along." She laughed at me before planting a kiss on my cheek.

Kupua motioned for us to sit. "Why don't we eat and catch each other up."

My stomach rumbled its appreciation as I settled on a cushion and reached for a piece of warm breadfruit, allowing it to melt in my mouth before swallowing, savoring every texture and flavor. I filled them all in with the details about what we'd learned about Donnie, their eyes popping as I confirmed he no longer slept in the chasm.

"Wow, I'm going to miss the big guy," Akalei said.

Kele shuddered. "Fo'real? Dat one scary bugga."

She smiled at him. "Yeah, but it wasn't his fault." She nudged her shoulder against his and he leaned in, kissing her cheek and nuzzling her with his nose. Eka watched them with longing and when she caught me looking at her, dropped her head, hiding her face under wild curls.

Kupua cleared his throat. "Destroying the flute was the only way to keep Henry from using it against us. Closing a portal to the Lua Pele's world can't be a bad thing, even if we don't understand exactly what happened to Donnie."

My future king, always the voice of logic. Admiration swelled in my heart for him. "So what's your news?"

"Moho's here, we captured him."

"What?" Eka screeched, shooting to her feet, scattering food everywhere and glaring at Kupua. "Where is he, did you hurt him?

Take me to him right now!" Fury shot like daggers from her eyes and her fists clenched, her mood swing causing my head to swim.

Kupua stood, throwing out his hands to reach for her but she quickly skittered out of his grasp. "We're keeping him in the healing room, and he's been treated in the healing pool. He's fine, just a flesh wound to his arm. My mother and Rachel have been tending to him."

My turn to be surprised. "Rachel's here?"

He nodded, shrugging. "When Moho snatched you I contacted Rachel right away. You know what she's like. If I hadn't told her, I'd never hear the end of it. She and my mother insisted on coming to help. Of course, that meant Mike had to come along as well. He won't let Rachel out of his sight, not with a baby on the way, the guys a little crazed."

Sounded about right. I stood and strode over to Eka, gently laying a hand on her shoulder, her muscles flinching under my touch. Softly, I spoke to her, "Eka, it'll be okay. No one will harm Moho. We'll take you to him right now, but can you calm down first? It won't help to have you agitated when you visit him."

Her shoulders slumped and her chest expanded as she took a deep breath. "I'm sorry...I trust you Tessa, I do. It's just...He's just...important to me. I want to make sure he's alright. Please, I have to see him."

"He's important to all of us," Kupua told her.

I gave Kupua a nod. "Let's go see him."

Moku-ola's healing room was located beneath the house and
197

underneath the waterfall feeding into the sacred pool of our city. A pipe caught water cascading off the waterfall, feeding into the healing pool, which constantly refreshed through a drain into the open sea. Thermal heat channeled from a nearby volcano warmed rock lining the pool, creating a soothing, bathwater-like temperature, perfect for facilitating recovery. Medicinal herbs added to the water assisted the healing process. Lavender permeated the room, creating a calming atmosphere so when you entered, stress oozed out your pores until you wanted to slump onto a bed and take a nap.

Off the main room, Kupua had established a locked recovery room in case we ever needed to contain a patient. He'd brought in plexiglass purchased from the surface to create a wide observation window, which came in handy now that Moho resided on site. A vent system allowed us to hear and speak to the occupant, like intercom systems in hospitals above the surface. A bed, bathroom and sink all provided more comfort than the cell he'd left me in back at Seamount, not that I was making comparisons, well, I tried not to anyway.

Eka rushed to the window, pressing her face against the glass like a child gazing into a pet shop window. "Moho, it's me, Eka."

Moho lay on his side, back to the window, motionless. He wore nothing but a pair of shiny, grey wetsuit pants and a bandage around one arm. His long black hair gathered into a tight ponytail at the nape of his neck. When Eka spoke, his shoulders tensed, but he didn't change position or respond.

"Please Moho…I want to help you. I love you."

Awkward silence swallowed us all, Kupua and Kele staring nervously at their feet, the wall and anything else besides the pitiful scene at the window. I gently touched Eka's shoulder. "Let him be for now, he may not be ready to speak to anyone," I whispered in her ear.

She jerked her shoulder away from my touch. "I'm not leaving him. I'll wait here until he's ready to talk. Leave us alone…please."

Kupua slid a chair over near the glass for Eka to use, waiting for me to respond. I had no idea what to do, but figured fighting her would take more energy than I could muster at the moment.

"Maybe we should leave them alone for now."

He nodded and we all retreated, leaving Eka alone with the man she loved; the man who wanted to destroy all we held dear.

CHAPTER 29

ALOHA AU IA'OE

I LOVE YOU

Hanging my head over the side of the bed, I checked on Sid, who still huddled inside his favorite shell in the moat. He waved and murmured a hello before tucking his tentacles neatly inside his cozy hiding spot. Stretching, I swung my legs onto the floor and forced myself upright. Tea...I needed jasmine tea, so I threw on some clothes and traipsed toward the kitchen. Outside my door Lizzy waited, a piece of driftwood sticking out either side of her mouth.

"Watcha have there?" I asked and wiggled the wood from between her teeth, kissing her nose and receiving a fishy, wet, slurpy nuzzle in return. Etched on the wood, in familiar handwriting, read; *meet me in the terrace room.* I smiled to myself, wondering what my sweetie might be up to and hoping it involved a cup of steaming jasmine tea.

The terrace room connected to the sacred pool and served as garden to the palace. Curved pools of water, terraced in shimmering levels climbed the walls from floor to ceiling, spilling water into one another, and draining into rows of plants growing in trenches circling along the floor. Harvested for both food and medicinal purposes, many of the plants were in various stages of growth and lovingly attended by experts living in the city. Pillows scattered throughout the large area, inviting visitors to sit and enjoy the peace and warmth. Air in the terrace sanctuary hung heavy with moisture, sweetened by flourishing herbs and flowers.

A stone corridor led to the terraces, smothered in moss and hanging vines. Turning the corner I gasped. Candles swarmed each pool, on every level, straight to the ceiling, showering soft light and flickering shadows throughout the area. Yellow hibiscus blossoms lined the pathway like lights on a runway, sweetening the air with their fragrance. In the center of the room knelt Kupua, his eyes brimming with emotion. He wore a garland of purple morning glories over a green silk tunic and pants, which stretched against his bulging muscles. A second garland draped in his hand, waiting for me. Next to him a blanket spread out with a banquet of my favorite foods, pineapple, breadfruit, grapes, hummus wraps, and to my delight, the scent of jasmine tea wafted in my direction like an invitation.

I slowly floated across the room to pause in front of him, my heart thumping against my chest. I ducked my head and held my breath as Kupua looped the lei around my neck, his fingers scooping hair out of the way. His eyes lit and his dazzling smile warmed me from inside out as he cocooned my hands in his.

"Your sister informs me it is customary to present a ring when making a marriage proposal. In Moku-ola it is customary to present a lei, a symbol of devotion and love. Today we honor both customs." My hand covered my mouth in surprise. He reached into a pocket and wiggled out a box. Opening it, he lifted it to me.

"This is the moment of sweet Aloha, I will love you longer than forever. Promise me your love in return, until the sun refuses to set and the waters run dry. Be my wife, join your spirit with mine under the Creator's blessing and I promise I will honor and cherish you as long as we both swim the seas."

Cradling the box in my hand, I collapsed to my knees, shaking, tears streaming down my cheeks. "Kupua, my heart, my love, belongs to you alone. Yes. I will be your wife." Emotion swelled my throat, making it difficult to say more. I'd already made my feelings known, promised to declare him king. But…this gesture went beyond, this was Kupua romancing me…and I hadn't even been aware I'd wanted him, too. But, I had, and his gesture erupted emotions buried deep within my soul.

He cupped my face in his hands, wiping away tears with his thumbs and rested his forehead against mine. "My sweet Ipo, you have no idea how much you mean to me. I would renounce the crown you offer in a heartbeat, it means nothing compared to your love. An O Ko Aloha Ka`u E Hi`ipoi Mau. With you, joy will ever be mine."

I sniffed, attempting to get my emotions under control so I could respond. After a pause, I squeezed his hands and spoke.

"Before I was queen, before I even knew what I wanted in life, there was you. From the moment I saw you, my heart changed, I changed. E Hookumu Maua Ka Hale Puni Maua Ohana Me Ka Pumehana A Me Ka Oiloli Kealoha. May we create a home that surrounds our family and friends with warmth, laughter and love."

He drew me tight against him and pressed his warm lips against mine, sending waves of warmth surging through me. Too soon he released me and removed the box from my grasp, plucking out a ring carved from polished green coral. Swirls ran through the thick band, mimicking waves of the sea. Taking my hand, he slid the ring into place, a perfect fit. He smiled. "My mother made us a matching set, I hope you like it."

I raised my hand, admiring the detail of the carving. "It's beautiful."

He shifted me onto the blanket and we settled next to the food. My stomach growled. I'd forgotten my earlier hunger and it returned with a vengeance.

"What are weddings like in Moku-ola? What are your traditions?" I asked, popping a grape into my mouth and swooping up a cup of tea off the platter.

"I've only been to one, Kele and Akalei's. Everyone in the city gets involved, quite a celebration, second only to birth celebrations."

"Birth celebrations?"

He raised an eyebrow at me. "Don't you have birth celebrations on the surface?"

"We have birthdays. Party's every year on the day we are born. Is that what you mean?"

He shook his head. "Not every year...on the actual *day* of the birth of one of our children. We celebrate the miracle and blessing of a new life joining our community. Every single person in Moku-ola assumes responsibility for caring for and protecting the child, who is beloved by all. There is no such thing as an orphan in our city. We each bring a gift for the parents, but not the kind of gifts you might be used to. Our gifts are our talents, which we pledge to share with the child. I often pledge to teach the art of carving driftwood, and Kele teaches how to care for wounds. This way our children learn from everyone."

His words sunk in. Once again the generosity and love of the people of Moku-ola awed me. "Wow. I wish people on the surface would show the same level of commitment to children. Maybe fewer would go hungry or be abused."

Confusion flitted across his face. "People allow children to go hungry?"

"Oh yeah. It's rough up there. And now, I'll have a little niece or nephew growing up there too." I already felt protective of Rachel's baby, and even though he or she hadn't been born yet, I wanted to erect a hedge of protection around the little tyke.

Kupua caressed my face with his finger, his expression softening. "We'll all look after Mike and Rachel's baby, she is one of us now too, part of our family."

I squinted my eyes at him. "What do you mean *she*? Have

some inside information you wanna share?"

He laughed. "No, just can't imagine a miniature Mike walking around, that's all, not sure the world is ready for two such characters."

An explosion boomed in the distance. Tremors shot through the floor and spilled water over the edges of the pool. I flung my hands out to prevent myself from tumbling backwards, spilling hot tea on the blanket.

I whipped my head toward Kupua. "What was that?"

He steadied himself. "Nothing good. If I didn't know better, I'd think we were under attack, but our only enemy is Moho and we have him locked away."

Blood rushed from my face. "He's not our only enemy."

CHAPTER 30

HOA PAIO

ENEMY

We bolted toward the center of the city where we could get the best view of the ocean overhead. Just as we converged on the pool, another blast rocked Moku-ola, knocking us off our feet. I landed on my hip with a thud, pain shooting up my side as I rolled to my knees. Kupua, grumbled next to me, rubbing his head and picking bits of rock from his hair. Gazing through the ceiling, I gasped. A tiger shark glided overhead, his jaws clenching a cylinder shaped metal object, which he released before flashing out of sight. As it floated toward us like a leaf falling from a tree, I braced myself and shouted to everyone within hearing range, "Hold on, another blast is coming!"

A loud crack shook the walls, pummeling homes and streets with volcanic rock. I glanced to Kupua as dread choked me. "Will the city survive intact under this assault? Do we need to evacuate?"

He frowned. "I'm not sure, we've never been under attack. I

don't think anything can penetrate the thick volcanic barrier to our city, but I'm not sure, this is our first bombing."

Great. Lots of firsts happening under my reign, only, not the good kind. How does one protect a city from bombs without hurting someone or risking damage to our precious ocean?

Crowds streamed toward the sacred pool as our people sought comfort and safety, their faces wrought with fear and confusion. Lizzy howled for my attention. I hauled myself to my feet, limping slightly from the bruise on my hip bone, which surely must be several shades of purple and green by now. She carried a message for Kupua and I. Slowly and carefully I eased my legs over the edge of the pool, favoring my non-damaged side, and dangled my feet into the water. Lizzy bobbed her head between my legs, setting her flippers on my thighs. I kissed her nose. "What news do you have for us?"

She nudged a note into my hand, wrapped in a plastic dry bag and left outside the entrance of the city. I plucked it from her mouth and unrolled it as Kupua sat beside me, looking over my shoulder. The paper was torn on the edges and the handwriting scribbled as if done in haste or anger. It read:

Release Moho now or I will continue to drop bombs on your city until it comes crumbling down around your feet. I will give you until sunset on the surface to decide. –Henry

My stomach turned over at his words, churning the contents, which threatened to come up. We could not lose the city, not now, not ever. The weight of Henry's ultimatum suffocated me, causing me to hyperventilate. Deep inside I knew destruction of the city was not the Creator's plan and I would do everything in my power to ensure the safety of the people of Moku-ola.

Kupua wrapped an arm around me, speaking softly into my ear. "He cannot destroy Moku-ola, its protection extends beyond the physical. Our Creator watches over us."

I relaxed slightly, hoping he was right because we couldn't let Moho go, but this craziness needed to end. We had to stop Henry's attack, and not by releasing Moho. One crazed lunatic on the loose seemed like enough to endure without adding the king of maniacs into the mix.

I rose and faced the group of people who'd gathered. "As you have felt, we are under attack, but do not despair, our Creator will protect us. The walls around us are strong and will not be crushed, just like our determination and courage. Kupua and I will find a way to stop the bombing. Please return to your homes and until we give the release, do not venture into the sea. Have faith." Heads bobbed in agreement as the crowd dispersed.

Kele and Akalei scrambled over to us from the other side of the pool. Weariness from all the conflict showed on the faces of my friends. "Let's go have a chat with Moho. I'm done playing games."

Eka still perched next to the plexiglass in the recovery room, her knees tight against her chest, curled in the corner. Nothing else seemed out of place, as if the blast hadn't reached this deep into our home. Moho lay with his back to us, unmoving. I crept over to Eka, crouching to speak face to face.

"Has he said anything to you?"

She shook her head back and forth, keeping her eyes downcast. "Not a word. I've tried to tell him I love him, would never betray him, but not a word." Pain sketched her features and my heart broke for her. "Do you think he'll ever forgive me? Ever love me again?"

I gently stroked her hair. "You did nothing wrong, there is nothing to forgive. Someday, when Moho accepts forgiveness himself, he will understand."

Cruel laughter from behind the partition interrupted our talk. I straightened and pivoted toward the glass. Moho spoke without changing positions. "She is not yours to comfort, Queen. You are naïve and have no understanding about what you speak of, so stop interfering and worry about your own kingdom and responsibilities…and how's that going by the way? I hear things are getting a little…shaky?"

Kupua and Kele maneuvered next to me, their shoulders brushing against mine, warm and reassuring. Eka dropped her head to her knees. Seeing her despair sent fury rolling through my veins. Akalei sat next to her and wrapped an arm around her shoulders. I narrowed my eyes at Moho.

"How long are we going to maintain this battle between us Moho? Isn't there some way to have peace, come to an agreement? Surely there's room enough in the ocean for us to live together without fighting? I don't know about you but I've got better things to do."

Slowly, he shifted his body off the bed and strode over to the plexiglass partition. Muscles flexed beneath the bandages still covering his arm as he stretched it out as if it no longer pained him. "Are you willing to turn the crown of Moku-ola over to me?"

I rolled my eyes and let out a sigh. "You know I can't do that. The crown has been given to me, it's not something I chose for myself. Besides, don't you have your own crown now? Or was that just a show for my benefit?"

His hands clenched into fists. "No show. I've been given a crown, but only one can rule the ocean. I am offering you the chance to join our powers. To be the most powerful rulers Moku-ola has ever seen."

His words sent chills down my spine, popping goose bumps out on my arms. "We don't serve the same power, you and I, and I will not betray mine. But, we can stop this fighting. Please Moho, let's live in peace."

Kupua clasped my hand and placed his other on the glass. "Brother, Tessa is right. Let's stop battling one another. Even if we cannot agree, we can at least come to a truce, leave each other to live in peace."

Moho dropped his head. "You disappoint me brother. You still haven't learned." He tilted his head to the side, glaring at Eka, who trembled under his stare. "You choose them over me? I turn my back and you run, then try to convince me you're loyal?" He spit on the floor, swiveled and flopped on his bed, his back to us once again.

Sadness hung in the air, heavy and tasting of defeat. My heart sank as reconciliation withdrew from my grasp, always just out of reach. If Moho wouldn't agree to live in peace, we could not release him, too many lives remained at stake. I leaned against Kupua, allowing his strength to gird me, renew me, his ocean scent filling me with calmness.

Kele whispered into my ear. "Moho suppa messed up and wops his jaws. Pay no attention."

"What are we to do about Henry and his bombs?" Akalei asked the question on all our minds.

Eka unfurled from her position in the corner. Her tiny body shaking as she spoke, like an electric wire on overload. "Release Moho. Queen Tessa, please, let him return to his own home and Henry will stop this craziness. Moku-ola will be safe if you let him go. Isn't that what you want?"

"No, Eka, releasing Moho won't make our city safer. Moho has made it clear he will not let us live in peace." I spoke softly, fearing she might lose her fragile grip on sanity at any moment. She bore so much pain for one so young. Looking into her eyes wrenched my heart. "Eka, you look exhausted. Let Akalei take you to your room to get some rest. Moho isn't going anywhere. You can come back once you've had some sleep and food."

She jutted her chin out in defiance. "No, I won't leave him again. I'm staying here."

"Don't do this, Eka, don't torture yourself."

She curled back into herself in the corner, keeping her eyes on the floor, her face haggard and weary.

211

I glanced from Kupua to Kele who shrugged helplessly. "Pua ting," (poor thing) Kele murmured under his breath.

I rubbed my head in frustration. "We should go somewhere private to talk, there are decisions to be made."

Moho's cruel laughter followed us out of the room, setting my nerves on edge. Reason and logic made no impression on him. Time to change tactics.

CHAPTER 31

ʻIMI

SEARCH

Sunset was fast approaching. Kupua, Kele, Akalei and myself joined Sid in a conference at the sacred pool. Since we clearly weren't releasing Moho, plan B had to be initiated. Too bad I didn't have a clue what plan B might entail.

Submerging beneath the warm water of the pool cleared my head as tension in my neck and arms softened. Sid wrapped his tentacles around my calf in an octo-hug, squeezing and massaging my strained muscles. Suction cups on his tentacles plucked at my skin, tickling, but better than any spa I'd ever visited. But today wasn't about relaxation; Sid had followed Henry after his last bomb drop and suggested a bold plan.

My three friends parked on the edge of the pool, dangling their feet, waiting as Sid explained his plan. I popped my head above the surface, wiping water from my eyes and licking salt from my lips. "Sid's got an idea I think might work, but it's risky. He's discovered where Henry's keeping the bombs and it's not far from Molokai. We can easily check it out. What do you think, time to play some offense?"

Kupua grinned as he heaved me out of the water onto the side of the pool, splashing himself in the process. "If it protects our city I'm always game. Just lead the way."

Akalei and Kele nodded. "Count us in."

We approached Molokai with caution, battling against strong currents and rip tides threatening to force us off course. Vertical sea cliffs rose like giants off the north shore and waves crashed with ferocity against the rocks. How Henry had managed to build an underwater bunker into the side of a cliff, here, baffled me and my respect for the guy grew, just a little.

Kupua traveled as a tiger shark, masking our scent with his own and concealing us in his shadow. His twenty-foot massive body cut through rough surge with little effort and we hung onto his tail, grateful for his strength, even if his sandpaper skin rubbed our hands raw. Surface dwellers avoided this area, reluctant to tangle with such a wild sea.

We'd only sensed one shark in the area, patrolling along the coast. My skin tingled as she crossed our path, just out of visual range, but radiating enough tension to send pulses throbbing against my skull. My skill at blocking out unwanted thoughts had vastly improved but she strummed on high alert, searching for intruders in her territory, operating under Moho's command. I held my breath until she cruised far enough away to ease the pressure in my temples and released a sigh, hoping there weren't more sharks coming.

Kupua led us deeper until we reached a massive granite door, three times the size of our entrance to Moku-ola, set into the immersed rock cliff of the island. Its grey surface blended with surrounding rock so well I might have missed it altogether if not for its glowing red hinges, spewing waves of heat through the currents. Closer inspection revealed a clear touch pad where a door handle might have been. I tentatively placed my hand over the touch pad, holding out little hope it would open. Nothing happened. How does one crack the code of a crazed lunatic?

Kele sidled next to me and nudged my shoulder. "Hoh, I memba da bugga Moho, he crazy 'bout da sharks. He only trust da sharks. Gef'um?"

Understanding slowly dawned on me. Of course, it made perfect sense. I motioned for Kupua to come closer to the door, moving aside to make room for his massive shape as a tiger. He slid between Kele and myself, his mouth slightly open, revealing rows of ragged teeth. I shuddered, despite knowing Kupua would never harm me, being this close to his form as a tiger shark made me tremble. Warm reassurance flowed into my heart, calming my nerves, as Kupua, sensing my reaction, responded with love.

Kele slapped Kupua on his dorsal fin, laughing. "I rekanotice you brah, even if you one scary brudda as da shark." He pointed to the touchpad. "You know wat to do."

Kupua bumped the pad gently with his nose several times as we held our breath, hoping Kele was right and the pad would respond to the touch of a shark. After several bumps the pad lit up in brilliant colors of purple, green and gold, shimmering in circular patterns. With a low rumble the door lifted from the bottom, like my parents old garage door, creaking and groaning. Ocean poured into the opening, sucking us along with its force until we crashed into the back of a small chamber. The pressure of water surging into the room pinned me against the rock wall, flattening my body.

Kupua morphed into human form, wrapping his arm around me as we smashed into the wall, helpless to stop the force of water claiming the small space. Kele and Akalei pressed against the smooth granite rock next to us, waiting, clinging to one another.

Kupua shouted above the thundering roar of water, "This must be an air chamber, there's got to be another door, a way into the main bunker."

I glanced around the room, searching for some clue to another exit while water rose over my head. Three identical walls of smooth marbled grey and white granite created the small air lock.

Finally, water reached the ceiling, calming, stabilizing and relieving the pressure holding us hostage so we could move freely. We ran our hands over the walls, confident a way in hid somewhere. The door rumbled once again, this time closing the small opening we'd entered through, blocking our only known way back into the sea. Panic surged up my throat until Kupua's calming touch focused me back on our task.

It wasn't long before a new vibration sent bubbles fizzing up from the chamber floor and water levels slowly dropped, draining ocean from our small enclosure. As soon as all water had emptied we collapsed to our hands and knees to scour the floor. To the eye, it appeared to be a smooth surface, devoid of any latch, handle or panel to open, but we knew eyes could be deceived. My hands felt like ice cubes as I passed them over the cold rock, being sure not to miss an inch of space. By the time I got to the far corner, I couldn't feel my fingers, they'd gone so numb searching the cold stone. Swiping them over a square of granite near the corner wall caused a high-pitched beeping to chime out. Bingo. Sensors in the floor, once dry, recognized movement and sent off a chain reaction as panels of rock underneath us shifted, slowly opening with a groan.

Kupua yanked Akalei's arm and tossed her against the wall just in time, as her foot dangled over empty space. "Stay back in the corner!"

Kele circled an arm around her waist. "Dis is so unz, wat we gonna do wen da whole floor gone?"

I watched how the panels shifted, dropped and receded under one another and pointed, getting everyone's attention. "I don't think the whole floor is moving, look, it's just the one section on each side."

Kupua leaned over, peering into the hole in the center of the room. I pushed to my feet, stretching out my cramped muscles and joined him.

About twenty feet below us hung a cache of missiles, stacked in neat rows waiting to be deployed. I paled. "Oh no...how are we ever going to get rid of all these before Henry comes back? There's just too many."

"Dis unreal," Kele whispered.

Akalei hovered next to him, her eyes big as saucers. Kupua stilled, as unmoving as a stone, hands on his hips and eyebrows scrunched into a frown. I knew that look and waited until he was ready to speak.

After several long moments he huffed. "Maybe we don't move them, maybe we just need to expose them?"

"Huh?"

He flashed his dimples at me, waving his hand at the missiles. "This can't be legal above the surface, right? The authorities wouldn't be too happy someone hid bombs here."

I nodded. "Definitely, not allowed."

"Right. Then all we really have to do is help the local police discover this place and they'll take care of the rest."

"Brilliant," Akalei said.

"Tessa, call Sid and instruct him to get Mike out here with his boat and scuba gear. He can radio the authorities about what he found while diving the area."

I smiled, Mike was about to become famous. Perfect.

CHAPTER 32

MEA PO'INO

DANGER

Mike anchored his boat at the coordinates we provided. His 25-foot fiberglass fishing vessel, named Ohana Kai (Ocean Family), rocked in the swells while he radioed his position and reported finding an illegal weapons cache. Scuba gear lay scattered on his deck to look like he'd just surfaced from a dive. Puna had come along for the fun, and ensconced himself on the cushioned bench consuming a sandwich. After all, one doesn't go out diving alone. We scouted the situation from a distance, bobbing just above the waves, making sure to keep out of sight.

A speedboat approached on the horizon, sleek and fast, its bow slightly raised as it cut through choppy waves. Kupua, back in shark form, shot forward toward Mike's boat, instructing me to wait behind. Another, smaller, female mako shark who'd been patrolling earlier also approached Mike's boat, in ever tighter circles. Mike seemed oblivious, speaking into his radio, arms waving intensely.

Unease skittered across my nerves, something didn't seem right about the approaching boat. No flags flew off its stern, which seemed odd, I was sure harbor police flew a U.S. flag. Sunset exploded brilliant orange and red streaks across the sky, slowly dimming the bright daylight, making it harder to distinguish features from a distance.

Dipping below the surface, I summoned nearby dolphins, trusting my instincts and not risking being caught unprepared, after all, trouble seemed to follow us like ants at a picnic. A local pod of spinner dolphin responded from the south side of the island, anxious to help their queen. Akalei, Kele and myself swam closer to Mike's boat and surfaced to get a better view of what was taking place.

Mike waved his arms at the approaching speedboat, leaping and shouting to get the attention of whoever stood at the helm. At the last minute the boat swerved, shooting a shower of spray in its wake, drenching Puna and his sandwich. Puna jumped to his feet, his face red, shaking a fist at the offending boat, his sandwich limp and soggy.

Below, Kupua hugged the hull of Mike's boat, keeping the female mako at bay. Her deference to his size registered in my senses, and she wasn't going anywhere near him.

Mike didn't recognize the man standing at the helm of the speedboat, he'd never met Henry, but I'd know him from any distance. He wore a baseball cap and Hawaiian shirt, not his usual attire but still, his sharp features were unmistakable. I sent Kupua a warning, my nerves prickling on edge, worried there was still no sign of the authorities. I wished for some way to warn Mike, but any attempts to get closer might reveal our presence.

Henry powered down his boat, launching buoys over the side to come alongside the Ohana Kai. He called out to Mike, "Hey there, everything okay? These are dangerous waters to be anchored, need any help?"

Puna stood shoulder to shoulder with Mike who shouted back his answer. "No worries, we've called the harbor patrol, they're on the way. Just a little engine trouble."

Smart Mike, letting Henry know police were coming. I held my breath, hoping Henry would buy Mike's story and stay out of the way. He scanned the horizon, squinting to pick out objects in the vanishing light before pivoting back to my brother in-law. "Looks like they might be a while, mind if I come on board and have a look? I'm pretty good at engine repairs."

Mike glanced at Puna and shifted his feet. Puna waved his arm at Henry. "Thanks brah, but I'm one of the best mechanics in Lanai and this engine's shot. Don't bother yourself, we'll be fine."

"No bother." Henry tossed a rope line over to Mike. "I'll bring over my tools. No harm in looking, right. I mean, what else you gotta do?"

Reluctantly, Mike caught the rope and Henry leapt onto the gunwale and hopped to the deck of the Ohana Kai, a toolbox in one hand. Puna met him nose to nose, using his bulky frame to send a subtle warning. "You have trouble hearing brah? We already called for help, and it'll be here soon. What's your deal?"

Henry threw up his free hand, backing a step. "Hey, I'm just trying to be friendly, I don't want any trouble."

Mike returned the rope to Henry. "No trouble. We just prefer to wait for our friends, don't feel right about strangers getting involved."

I didn't like the direction this was taking and dove deep, Kele and Akalei following close behind, moving under Mike's boat, preparing for trouble. Whatever Henry had planned, I couldn't allow any harm to come to Mike, not if I ever wanted to face my sister again. Kupua shifted position to make room for us, rising closer to the surface and circling the boats. I huddled directly beneath the hull, my hands pressed against the hard fiberglass surface, listening to the voices murmuring above.

"Listen, you don't want my help, fine." The boat rocked slightly as someone, presumably Henry, stepped onto the gunwale. "Hey, how's the diving around here anyway? My brother wanted me to scope it out for a future dive."

Sounds in the distance distracted me. My dolphins were close, waiting for further instruction. Farther away, a motor roared, its increasing volume suggesting it headed our way – hopefully the harbor patrol. I asked the dolphin to establish a perimeter around our location and keep any sharks from entering. No way to know what Henry might try, and history told me he wouldn't give up easily.

Suddenly, the boat rocked violently above us and sounds of a fight thundered through the hull, shouting and stomping echoing above us. Then Mike shouted, "Watch out brah, he's got a gun!"

Kele immediately rocketed to the surface, hauling himself onto the boat to join in the fray. Swallowing my fear for Mike, I swam to the aft and scrambled onto the swim board, Akalei at my shoulder.

Gunshots blasted through the commotion and the stench of gasoline assaulted the air. Ocean turned slick as fuel poured into the sea from a hole in the tank. My nose burned as vapors rose from the surrounding water, spewing deadly poison into my precious ocean. I directed Sid to plug the hole, knowing he could handle it and shifted my attention to the fight on deck.

Mike, Henry and Puna locked together in a tangled mass of limbs and bodies, struggling for possession of the gun. They writhed across the deck, bumping, grunting and sweating, finally becoming pinned against the port side of the boat. Kele frantically tied knots into nylon rope, his fingers a blur of speed. He glanced over at us and shouted, "No make. Get down. No try me tita, da brah got a gun! We canna let you get hurt!"

Akalei tugged me to the floor. "He's right Tessa, let Kele handle it. We can't risk you getting shot."

I shook off her grip, determination burning my chest. "Sorry, but that's my brother in law and it's my job to protect all of you, remember." Before she could reply I swung my leg over the stern and rolled onto the deck, crouching low on my hands and knees.

Kele shot me a furious glare and pounced into the struggle, his hands working quickly to tie rope around Henry's feet. With two quick loops he leapt backwards and yanked on the other end of the rope. "Mike, Puna, maka flip an get off him!"

Mike and Puna sprang away as Henry's feet catapulted into the air and the gun skidded across the deck, within my reach. I scooped it into my hand and pointed it at Henry who now hung upside down from a rope Kele had anchored to the flying bridge.

"Let me down, this is outrageous," he cried out, flailing his arms, attempting to grab onto anything within reach.

"We'll release you as soon as the harbor patrol gets here, then you can explain all those missiles hidden below."

He stilled as the reality of his predicament sunk in.

Kele glared in my direction. "Why you did dat? You couldda got shot, usamara you?"

I lifted my chin as Kupua leapt over the starboard side of the boat, landing in front of me, facing Kele. "Kele, you know better than to question your queen. It's right for her to fight for her family, her people."

Kele's eyes glassed over and his head dropped. "Forgive me my queen, I used fo' protecting and forget."

"It's okay, Kele, I know you want me to be safe, but I can't just stand back and watch you all risking your lives without helping. What kind of a queen does that?" I gently laid my hand on Kupua's shoulder and he spun toward me, arms open. I flung myself into his arms, letting out a sigh of relief as his warmth enfolded me. Looking over his shoulder, I could see the approaching patrol boat. Finally, help on the way.

"We'd better vanish underwater before the patrol boat gets

here. Mike, you got this?"

He nodded. "Yeah Kika, I got this. Get outta here."

I blew him a kiss, before plunging into the sea, calling over my shoulder, "Don't let all the fame go to your head now. I don't want to have to come rescue you from Rachel!"

Deep laughter chased me into the ocean, melting like warm chocolate through my veins, spreading warmth into my heart.

CHAPTER 33

PU'IWA

SURPRISE

Beneath the waves, Kupua transformed into a dolphin and I climbed onto his smooth, sleek back. Kele and Akalei latched onto his tail, all of us anxious to return home.

"Hey, Tessa, now that we've dealt with Henry and his bombs, what d'ya say we have some fun? Maybe do something to celebrate?" Akalei teased.

"Do I dare ask what you have in mind?"

Her eyes gleamed with mischief. "Somewhere you haven't been yet…a surprise."

I sighed, not sure whether to be worried or excited, but certain I'd never want to disappoint my friend, and patted Kupua's side. "Yippee, a surprise. Okay sweetie, show us the way."

It wasn't far, which was a surprise because I'd thought I'd seen everything in the Hawaiian waters. A few miles off the Kauai coast, at a depth of several hundred feet, a brilliant coral arch loomed, bright with pink, blue, yellow, purple and green swirling colors. Bubbles fizzed within the arch, forming a screen we couldn't see past.

We floated just outside the screen of bubbles. I twisted toward Akalei. "What now?"

She smiled and clasped Kele's hand. "This is Kings Coral Arch. Only those in the presence of a king are able to see the arch. Nobody's been here since Kupua's father died."

I tilted my head, rubbing my eyes. "Why can *we* see it? I'm not a king."

"No, but the moment you named Kupua to the crown, he became one."

Stretching out, I rested my head against Kupua's smooth back, running my hands across his side, as warmth bubbled inside me.

Akalei continued. "Our people speak of one true King who created this arch so future generations might have a place to seek guidance and blessing. Kupua can lead us through the arch."

Slowly, Kupua advanced through fizzing bubbles that tickled as they popped against my skin. Time stood still as we passed beneath pink coral as if it no longer existed, transporting us independent of time and space. I caught the familiar fragrance of cinnamon, soothing my senses with comfort and peace. Reaching, I grazed a piece of coral to discover it had no substance, my fingers passing through the swirl of colors, which quickly fell back into form.

On the far side of the arch, we no longer swam in a sea but rested on cushions of velvet clouds. Beneath me Kupua transformed into human form, sending us both tumbling across the billowy surface and landing in sitting positions among the puffy clouds. My hands stroked the soft wisps in wonder as they both held my weight and appeared to be without substance or form, evaporating through my fingers into vapors.

Every cell in my body tingled with awareness, I'd never felt so alive, so in tune with my purpose. Bright light basked us each in its glow, radiating love. I leaned backwards on my hands, closing my eyes, tilting my face into the light and absorbing peace. Around me, my friends were doing the same, each lost in their own experience.

A voice echoed in my ears. *Well done, faithful servant.*

My heart swelled, overflowing with every emotion I'd ever felt, as if those few words invoked knowledge of events beyond my human comprehension, providing a glimpse into the heavenly arena. Blood running through my veins heated, warming me from the inside out. I tried to speak but no words crossed my tongue, yet all thoughts felt acknowledged, understood. The Creator knew every corner of my being, every decision, care and worry. I laid them all at His feet. Tears streamed like rivers down my cheeks as a testament to my joy at knowing and being known. My body felt lighter than feathers as burdens lifted, released off my shoulders and I floated in the Creator's caress.

I had no idea how long we basked in His glow; maybe a few minutes, maybe a lifetime. It didn't matter. All I knew was as warmth and light faded, drew distant, its loss stung and I wanted it back. My body went limp as if my limbs were suddenly made of jello, loose and floppy.

I opened my eyes and stared into Kupua's face, poised directly above me, dimples popping on the sides of a huge grin, and I stroked his cheek.

"Wow, that was amazing!"

He grasped my hand in his and pulled me upright into a sitting position, my legs crossed in front of me. "What did you hear?"

"He said, *well done,* and it made me feel as though he and I were the only two in the universe."

He nodded and glanced over to Kele and Akalei who scooted closer to join us. "How about you two?"

Akalei wiped tears from her face, shaking her head and avoiding my gaze. Kele rubbed her shoulder and said, "Da King of kings say he giv me gift of healing an my turn fo' take da keikis to train dem, prepare dem fo healing to. He say I da bomb. How bout you brah?"

Red flushed Kupua's cheeks. "He anointed me as protector of the queen, and warrior for the sea." Kupua ran a hand through his hair and sheepishly looked at me out of the corner of his eye. "Hope you don't mind having a protector."

Warmth curled around my heart. "You already have my heart to protect, might as well include the rest of me."

He squeezed my hand and bumped his forehead against mine.

Thoughts whirled through my brain, attempting to wrap around what just happened. "What is this place?" I turned my head to smile at Akalei. "How did you know to come here?"

She leveled her tear stained face in my direction. "You named me your royal guard when you were crowned, remember?" I nodded, that day forever etched in my memory, being crowned isn't something one forgets. "Well…the people of Moku-ola all know of the Kings Coral Arch but none know when or where it might appear until it's revealed to the appointed royal guard of the ruling house. When you named Kupua your king, even though he has yet to be crowned, I prepared my heart to receive information about where and when to bring you both here. I had no idea what would happen when we arrived, I only followed directions given to me in the moment. The King of kings has blessed your union by bringing you here before the crowning ceremony, usually the Kings Coral Arch appears after, but you two have been tested more than most."

"That's an understatement," I said. "Akalei, can you share what you heard?"

She let out a sigh and straightened. "Sorry, it was a bit overwhelming because I didn't just hear words but felt the emotions of others." Her words thickened with emotion. "He showed me the value of encouraging and loving others and why he blessed me with such gifts. He allowed me to feel what others feel when they are loved and supported." She paused and let out a sob, tears flowing once again. "He showed me what a difference my loving others makes…and I had no idea, never guessed at what it truly meant."

Kele wrapped his arms around her, pressing her tight against his chest. I took a deep breath and exhaled the emotions building in my own throat.

"So this is meant to encourage us, help us grow stronger?"

Kupua flashed his smile, clearly soaring from his experience. "Yeah, pretty awesome isn't it."

"Can we come back or is this a one-time deal?"

Akalei shook her head. "Don't know. You can't ask for it, it's a gift."

"Pretty incredible gift."

Akalei wiped her tears with the back of her hand, sniffling. "Yeah, hard to top this one. But…what I don't get is how could we not know, what kept us from understanding our worth before?"

Kupua grunted. "Don't know about you, but I've been focused on other things, like how to stop my brother from destroying our city."

I leaned forward. "That's part of it, but, I know I've also had doubts, like maybe someone else could do a better job, or I wasn't good enough. Maybe this is a wake-up call, reminding us to walk confidently and not second-guess ourselves. Seems like He knew exactly what we needed."

Kele scratched his head, whispering, "Wow, dis crazy good."

"You're right about that Kele. We can't let each other ever forget, agreed?"

Everyone chimed together, "Agreed." In that moment, it felt like bonds between us cemented, linking our hearts forever in love and friendship.

Kupua rose like a king, tall and confident. "Time to head home."

I gazed around my feet at billowy clouds, suddenly surrounded with a rainbow of colors, hesitating, not wanting to leave. Kupua drew me closer.

"They say this is just a taste of what the afterlife will bring in heaven, but we must look forward, our work here in the sea is not yet done." His breath tickled my ear as he spoke into it, sensing my hesitation.

He was right, others depended upon us, waited for us to return. Maybe our experience would help us encourage our people to understand their value as well, share in this new awareness. Akalei took my free hand in hers, sending strength and assurance flowing through my veins like wildfire, reminding me I didn't have to do anything alone, we were all united. I led us back through the Kings Coral Arch, ready to deal with whatever waited in the deep blue sea.

CHAPTER 34

MAKANA

GIFT

We entered Moku-ola sometime during the middle of the night, refreshed, calm, peace covering us like a warm blanket but ready for some hard-earned sleep. Kele and Akelei headed straight for their room, hand in hand, blissed out. Kupua veered off toward the kitchens hoping to grab a quick bite to eat, leaving me alone, gazing out over the sleeping city of Moku-ola.

Lizzy welcomed me by waddling over as I surveyed my city from the main floor and nuzzled my hand with her cold, wet nose. I stroked her silken neck, warming my hands against her slick fur. Below, lights dimmed, tide pools stilled and a distant swooshing of a few young men sweeping debris the only sound echoing through the city. I enjoyed the quiet, knowing in two days we'd be announcing my decision to crown Kupua and setting a date for the event…and our wedding. The people of Moku-ola relished a good celebration.

I decided to check on Eka before crashing into my bed,

hoping to put my nagging unease about her welfare to rest. I found her camped out in the same spot, next to Moho's window, snuggled in a sleeping bag, her curly hair poking from under the zipper. As I turned to close the door and let her sleep, her head popped up, knuckles rubbing her half-awake eyes.

"You're back. Everything okay?"

"Yeah, it's all good. I'll let you sleep."

"It's okay. I'm awake now, I'd like to hear what happened."

I glanced over at the window, Moho appeared to be sleeping but I couldn't be sure. "How about you come to my room, we can talk in private."

She squirmed out of her sleeping bag and followed me through the hall, yawning and combing fingers through her wild mass of hair.

Lizzy barked as we entered my room before settling into her favorite sleeping spot by the moat. She groaned and fidgeted until discovering the right position, and plopped her head on the pillow.

I burrowed into my comfy bed, propping myself on several pillows. Eka perched on the edge, back straight, biting her nails. I tossed a pillow at her and patted the spot next to me. "Get comfy and let's talk."

A smile lit her face and her body relaxed as she crawled under the blankets and leaned against a soft pillow. "Thanks, Queen Tessa."

"Just Tessa, we're friends. Now tell me how you're doing…really."

Shadows passed over her face. "Moho's talking to me now, that's good, right?"

"Depends on what he's saying."

She bit on another nail. "He's not all bad, I know he still loves me, he's just angry."

"Eka, just because he loves you doesn't mean he has the right to hurt you or disrespect you. True love forgives, is kind and selfless."

She covered her face with her hands. "You don't understand, I can't walk away, I just can't."

I released a sigh and changed the subject. "Okay, how about I tell you what happened tonight."

She flipped on her side and nodded, while I relayed all the events leading to Henry's arrest. By the time I finished, her eyes drooped, fighting to stay open. I pulled the covers over her shoulders and whispered. "Get some rest, we can finish talking in the morning." She mumbled something and rolled onto her stomach. I curled on my side and drifted off to sleep.

Screams rang through the ocean but I couldn't find the source. I searched strange waters, diving deep, only to hear cries in another direction. Someone or something needed my help. Frantic, I swam farther from home, desperate to discover the source of the anguished cries. Darkness pressed in, decreasing visibility but still I swam. Approaching the ocean floor, I caught a glimpse of movement, a figure struggling in pain. Swimming closer to investigate, I found a shark, dying, blood seeping from its gills. I reached my hand out in comfort when it twisted around and clamped onto my hand with its jaws, sending searing pain through my...

I bolted upright in bed, pain jolting me from sleep, my arm aching. Sweat-matted hair flattened against my neck, and it took a moment to catch my breath. Rubbing my arm, I realized it was just a dream. I glanced over at Eka, to find her spot empty and cold, wondering how long she'd been gone.

Looking up, I gasped: beautiful birds of paradise, my favorite flower, filled my room, their bright orange, yellow and red plumes in brilliant display, scenting the air with floral aromas. Around my bed stood life size carvings of sea lions, dolphins, sea turtles and an octopus.

I scratched my head and wondered what was going on when Rachel and Kupua cracked the door open. My sister's face lit when she saw I was awake and she burst in, carrying more gifts in her arms, or rather on top of her now prominent belly. "Happy Birthday, little sis!"

I groaned and fell on my pillows. I'd completely forgotten it was my birthday.

Akalei and Kele trailed behind my sister and Kupua, crowding the bed. Rachel sat next to me on the edge, gifts tumbling out of her arms. "Come on Tessa, be a good sport and let us help you celebrate."

I swung my legs off the bed and hugged her. "Okay, okay, I'm up." I stood and padded over to one of the wood carvings, running my fingers along the polished surface and grinned at Kupua.

"These are beautiful, I love them."

He ducked his head, smiling. "Good. I wanted to surround you with friends while you slept."

Tears pushed against my eyes, threatening to spill, as my heart swelled. I shut my eyes and covered them with the backs of my hands, trying not to lose it. He took the few steps between us and wrapped his arms around me, kissing my head. "What's wrong?"

I sniffed. "Nothing, it's perfect. I don't know why I'm crying."

He squeezed tighter.

Rachel cleared her voice. "Well, not that *I* want to compete with Mr. Perfect, but there are more gifts over here."

"Yeah brah, don't hog da show."

Kupua released me and I hopped to the bed. Rachel handed me a flat square present, then suddenly inhaled and clutched her stomach. "The baby kicked!"

My breath caught. "Really, can I feel?"

She guided my hand over the spot on her tummy she'd been holding. "Here, wait..."

I held my breath in wonder, until something inside my sister stirred and thumped against my hand. Emotions choked me, and my heart sped, a true miracle fluttered inside her, unfathomable and yet, familiar. "I felt her! Or is it a him?"

She shook her finger at me. "No, no...we don't want to know until the little one is born, Mike and I want it to be a surprise."

I frowned at her. Akalei nudged me on the bed. "Can I feel

237

the baby?"

Rachel scooted toward her. "Of course, baby's pretty excited right now. Put your hand here." Rachel shifted Akalei's hand to the spot I'd just been touching.

Akalei squealed with delight when the baby kicked against her hand, unaware of our joy at his or her antics. Rachel motioned at me. "Aren't you going to open your present?"

"Oh, yeah, sorry…but it's going to be hard to top feeling my niece or nephew kick." I ripped the paper and stared at an engraved picture frame holding a shot of Rachel, myself and our mom, taken not long before her death. We had our arms around each other and were laughing, not even looking at the camera. We'd been walking along a pier in southern California, laughing at some stupid joke Rachel had told. My dad liked to capture candid pictures and he'd snapped this one without us knowing. I'd almost forgotten that day. Engraved under the picture was *A hui hou,* until we meet again.

Rachel's eyes matched my own, glassy with tears. "Best…gift…ever." I threw my arms around her neck and we held one another, squeezing tight. I whispered in her ear, "Thanks sis, you always know what I need."

Kele grunted behind us. "Okay, dat one chokin gift. Now open dis one." He pushed a small box tied with dried seaweed into my hand.

"It's from both of us," Akalei said.

I slid the seaweed aside and peered inside the box where a locket made from polished abalone shell hung from a string of tiny green seashells. I lifted it from the box to examine closer and it opened, revealing a picture of my mom and dad.

"Rachel gave us the picture and Kupua's mom made the necklace, but it was our idea," Akalei whispered.

Once again, words stuck in my throat. How did they all know exactly what would mean the most to me? I opened my arms wide for a group hug, embracing both Kele and Akalei in one swoop. "Thank you both, it means so much to me."

Akalei pulled back and smiled. "There's more. Since you know how everyone likes to celebrate, we've moved your announcement to tonight so the people of Moku-ola can be part of both your birthday and announcement. They wouldn't want to be left out, hope it's okay."

I stepped back and grasped Kupua's hand. "I'm ready, what about you?"

His eyes sparkled. "Oh yeah, let's do it!"

"I suppose you have everything planned, Akalei?"

Rachel slowly rose, holding her tummy with one hand and her back with the other. "Hey, she had some help, I'm not about to miss this either."

I knew in that moment, this was special, a memory I'd recall later and re-run in my head, cherishing every word and smile from my family, knowing we shared a bond of love. Nothing grand, just us, in my room, together and comfortable, was the best gift I could have received.

CHAPTER 35

NUHOU

NEWS

"Has anyone seen Eka?" I asked the group as we gathered by the sacred pool, preparing to announce our engagement and Kupua's upcoming crowning.

Kupua shrugged. "Haven't seen her since we got back, she's probably still holding vigil with Moho."

I bobbed on my tip-toes, scanning the crowd for her curly head. "She promised to come."

Akalei's eyebrows scrunched together. "Do you want me to go find her?"

"No, we don't have time. I'm sure she'll show up." I adjusted my headpiece, and ran fingers over my hair, making sure everything was still in place. I wore an emerald gown beaded with mother of pearl to match my crown. Around my neck hung the strand of black pearls Kupua had given me when we'd first met, and on my hand, the ring he'd presented when he proposed. I'd asked his mother to

240

custom make another so I could put its match on his hand when we married. I'd also set her to work on his future crown, something special I'd designed myself, a surprise.

Kupua wore a shimmering, emerald tunic with long pants, tied at the waist with a belt beaded with mother of pearl to match my gown. His normally shaggy, black hair was trimmed and styled thanks to Akalei, and when he flashed his dimples at me, my knees threatened to fold.

Kele and Akalei wore traditional purple signifying their role as our royal guard. Akalei's dress poofed out in layers of varying shades, cascading around her ankles. Her long black hair wrapped in a braid, laced with purple seashells.

People of the city all wore green to honor my birthday. Together, they formed an indoor sea, flowing like water moving around the pool. Each shouted greetings and well wishes as they passed, hoping to find a spot to best hear our announcement. Gratitude swelled in my chest at the love rushing over me, lifting my spirits.

Above us a calm ocean swirled in the ceiling, where various fish gathered to watch from their bird's-eye view. I waved, sending several trumpet fish into a tizzy, spinning in circles. Lizzy, Mimi, Ka, Sid, Rico, and Fin all splashed about in the sacred pool as honored guests, accepting food from children camped along the edge. Giggles and laughter rang through the city, warming me to the bone.

The glass platform hovered in the center of the pool, and

we'd added steps to a raised glass stand so more of our people could see us as we spoke. The city itself boasted perfect acoustics for speeches or music events: no microphones needed.

Kupua extended his hand to me. "Ready?"

I twined my fingers with his and strode onto the glass platform, his strength settling my nerves. "Always." Together we swung to face our beloved people, able to see every friend from our raised platform. I recognized most of the faces, young, old, filled with expectation and beaming with smiles that warmed my chest and pushed tears against my eyes. I inhaled the sweet, fresh aroma unique to my underwater home. Kupua and I raised our joined hands for all to see, and cheers blasted off the rock walls.

I beamed at the sea of affection before us. As I spoke, the crowd quieted until nothing could be heard but my words. "Kupua and I care for you all so much and want to share our special news with you, our family. We love each other and have decided it's time to make a commitment. We plan to marry in a few months, and I am formally announcing Kupua will be crowned your king." Shouts and cheers erupted and Fin flicked his tail showering us with water.

Kupua lifted his hand and the crowd hushed once again. "Today we also celebrate Queen Tessa's birthday, and in honor of this occasion, our family from the surface, Mike and Rachel, have music to share."

Kupua and I hopped from the platform and I kissed Rachel on the cheek as she and Mike took our place. Mike lugged his guitar and a chair, which he arranged for Rachel to be comfortable. She eased into it slowly, one hand on the smooth wood back for balance. Once settled, Mike began to strum and Rachel's voice lifted in song, her soft melody carrying through the city, enrapturing the people of Moku-ola.

Scanning the area I glimpsed a curly head as Eka appeared out of the crowd, her eyes swollen and red, tears still wet on her face. I reached for her arms, tugging her closer. "Eka, what's wrong, why are you crying?"

"I have to talk to you and Kupua, alone, now…please."

I motioned her over to an alcove behind the waterfall, away from the mass of people. Dread rose like bile in my stomach, this couldn't be good. Once we all crammed into the small area I turned to her. "Okay, we're as alone as we're going to get today. What's going on?"

She let out several sobs, struggling to get her words out. "I'm so sorry…I hope you can forgive me."

Kupua tensed next to me, his muscles rigid and tight. I placed my hands on Eka's shoulders. "Eka, you have nothing to fear from us. Forgive you for what? What's happened?"

Her hands started flailing about as she spoke. "I couldn't help it. I never wanted anyone to get hurt. I didn't know what to do."

Kupua growled in frustration and I elbowed him, Eka didn't need any more pressure, her body already vibrated like a live wire. "Take a deep breath Eka, it's alright, just calm down and tell us."

She stopped and inhaled deeply, fixing her gaze on me. "I let Moho go free."

My mouth dropped open as my arms began to shake, shock rocking my will to remain calm. "Moho's loose in the city? Why would you do something like that?"

"I couldn't help it, I love him. There's good in him Tessa, I know it. He's going to be the father of my child and he said if I didn't free him, we'd never be together." She wrung her hands and avoided my gaze.

I did a double take, certain I'd misheard her statement. "What did you say?"

She stared at her feet, shuffling from one to the other and whispered, "I'm pregnant."

CHAPTER 36

MOHO KU'OKO'A

FREEDOM

Stretching out my arms and legs, I reveled in the warm ocean currents flowing across my skin in welcome embrace. Hanging with one hand off the back of Nikko's tail fin, we rocketed towards Seamount to regroup, drunk with the high of newfound freedom. Fish fled at our approach, scattering in different directions in their weak attempt to confuse us, as if that would work. Today, our hunger burned for vengeance, not dinner.

Groaning in my stomach brought my thoughts back to Eka and her last minute decision to release me from Tessa's prison. It'd taken her long enough and her delayed loyalty weighed like bricks in the pit of my gut. So much for love conquering all. Her hesitancy would have to be dealt with at some point but now I had other, more pressing issues. A deep fire demanding to be quenched by revenge burned in my stomach.

According to Eka, Henry'd been arrested and waited for my rescue above the surface. If I didn't need some of his unique talents, it wouldn't matter, but that stupid fool had skills even I couldn't replicate. He may no longer have the flute, but there were other tools at his disposal Tessa hadn't seen and I required their use to ensure my total domination of the sea.

A growl exploded from my chest and I swung my body onto Nikko's back, spurring him faster toward my volcano. Action; I yearned for action. Too long had I languished in Moku-ola.

Turbulence quaked through the sea, waves building and pounding the surface as we approached Seamount. Surging currents churned through the waters as if the ocean itself angered in sympathy to my plight.

Nikko passed beneath the underwater entrance to my new home and I leapt off his back into my pressurized tunnel. The moment my feet touched ground I felt the Lua Pele's summons, thrumming through my veins, sizzling my insides and wrenching me toward the throne room like a magnet. Nothing could resist the call, not once it seeped into your veins and blackened your heart with a poison so thick it became a fortress against conflicting emotions like love and compassion. My first time, I'd responded out of curiosity more than anything, but now, I knew who I belonged to and where I owed my fealty.

Jogging, I reached the throne room in seconds, the blast of heat knocking me back a step and the strong odor of sulfur burning my lungs. Pain became nothing but something to endure, another test of my worthiness to be king. I perched on my throne and waited for the Lua Pele.

Steam, chased by sparks, spewed from the fissure, weighing heavy in the air like a thick winter coat. Clothing clung to my skin as temperatures spiked and steam sizzled, raking against my skin and leaving angry, red welts. I grit my teeth, prepared to endure all the Lua Pele had planned. I'd failed, earning the Lua Pele's wrath and I knew better than anyone what such wrath meant.

Clutching the sides of my throne, my body tensed for pain, every muscle taut with expectation. Searing, red-hot pokers ripped open flesh along my thigh, shooting scorching pain up my leg. Inhaling the stench of my own burning flesh, I ground my teeth, offering no resistance. Another slash along my back and a scream of agony caught in my throat, threating to tear lose despite my control. Blood trickled down my back and leg, mixing with sweat and dripping onto the steaming floor with a crackling sound. I shook my head, spraying sweat into the air as another rip tore through my side, deeper than the others, teetering me on the edge of a breakdown. *How much more must I endure?*

My chin dropped against my chest, the strain of keeping it raised no longer worth the effort. Sweat and blood clouded my vision and I closed my eyes to shut it all out as steam cleared around me, leaving a slight drop in temperature in its wake.

A raspy voice whispered in my ear. *It will not go so easy if you fail again. You must pass the test or die. I will find another to*

247

take your place, make no mistake. If you want to keep this kingdom, you must not fail. Now...what is it you wish to ask of me?

I licked my lips, the metallic tinge of my own blood stinging my throat. "I'm ready to offer the sacrifice."

Cackling rippled across the room. *You swear to offer royal blood, here, on my throne?*

"Yes, but don't forget your promise if I do. You will gift me the ability to wield Henry's weapon and supply the power you have withheld."

You agree to turn over your own blood relative to me?

"Yes."

Laughter echoed off the walls, piercing my ears. *Done, my king. Once the sacrifice is made, here on my throne, then you will have all you ask.*

I shuddered. Steam sucked back into the fissure, taking with it heat and fire, leaving me exhausted and shaken, slumped against the back of the throne. My heart hardened against my chest as I focused on my new task, refusing to face the turmoil of emotions swirling within. Confusion clouded my vision as thoughts and emotions collided within my soul. Somewhere, in the recess of my mind a voice called, urging me to turn from the path I'd set in motion, claiming to love even me. Slamming down walls all around this voice, this intruder, I straightened. No turning back, I'd made my choice. Only one thing mattered in this moment, I must retrieve Henry, the key to unlocking my power and crushing Moku-ola.

CHAPTER 37

TESSA

NA'AUAO

WISDOM

Kupua and I plopped to the sandy ground of the same deep sanctuary hole we'd found refuge in during the tsunami. Shifting sand crunched under our feet, echoing off high ceilings, harsh in comparison to the still silence of the cavern. Calmness flowed over my mind like the gentle music of a lullaby, every muscle releasing and turning to jello.

We sought peace, quiet, and solitude for prayer, guidance, and wisdom regarding how to protect our kingdom without losing Moho to darkness forever. Responsibility weighed heavy on my shoulders, a burden I felt grateful not to carry alone. Kupua enfolded my hand in his as we settled in the sand, reclining against the smooth volcanic rock for support.

"There's a way, Kupua. I know the Creator will show us how

to reach Moho. He will not be lost forever."

His chin fell against his chest, eyes focusing on grains of sand speckling his feet crossed in front of him. "I know you're right, but it's hard to hold onto hope after so long. I'm tired of all the pain. How much longer do we have to wait?"

"Hey, pain's a consequence of Moho's selfish choices, but it's not who he was created to be. All we have to do is somehow get through to the Moho you knew and loved as a child. He's still there, somewhere. I've seen glimpses of him."

His voice cracked. "How can you be so sure?"

"Because the Creator found me, even when I didn't know I was lost. The same can happen for Moho, I know it's possible. We have to be patient and believe."

His eyes softened, glistening with tears. "I love you, Tessa. It means the world to me you haven't given up on my brother, even when I have my own doubts, you have faith."

My voice shook as I whispered, "I wish I had answers, but I'm at a loss about what to do next."

A smile lifted one side of his face. "That's why we're here, right? For answers."

I closed my eyes and pressed my forehead against his, allowing silence to wrap us in its cocoon. Thoughts drifted as I focused my heart toward the Creator. I listened in faith for answers about how to save Moho.

Soft wisps of warmth caressed my neck, tingling my skin and spreading along my shoulders and arms, cradling me in an embrace.

I inhaled the sweet cinnamon scent associated with being in His presence. I exhaled and released my mental grip on physical surroundings, fully submitting myself to listening. His voice caused time to cease, and even Kupua's hand covering mine failed to register in my awareness. I was safe, valued and loved. New knowledge soaked deep into my brain, wisdom beyond my own imagining, and understanding as foreign and familiar as its source. Insight solidified as an idea grabbed hold of my thoughts like a leash restraining a tiger.

Slowly, cinnamon faded and a chill replaced the warmth wrapped around me. I straightened my back, stretching and waking to my surroundings.

Kupua's soft eyes met mine. "The answer is so simple, how did we miss it?"

I shook my head. "Don't know." Running my fingers through my hair, my thoughts cleared. "We have two brothers to save, not just one. Better get to work."

PIDGEN GLOSSARY

Ackshaun – action

FOB – Fresh off the boat

Brah/Braddah – good friend

Broke da mouth – good food

Fo'real – are you serious?

Grinds – food for eating

Habut – mad

Howzit – Hello, how's it going?

Huhu – mad

Lolo – crazy

Shark bait – someone who does not go in the sun and skin stays white

Tita or Teeta – term of affection, little sister

Coming Soon:

Book 3 in the

ABOUT THE AUTHOR:

Dr. Tara Fairfield is a licensed psychologist with over twenty years of experience working with youth and families. The mother of three children, Dr. Fairfield is dedicated to helping struggling teens find their confidence and faith in the Lord. She currently lives in Washington State where she can be close to her family and smell the salty air of the Puget Sound.

www.TaraFairfield.com

www.MakaiQueen.com

Twitter: @MakaiQueen

Makai King is proudly published by:

Creative Force Press

www.CreativeForcePress.com

Do You Have a Book in You?

www.ingramcontent.com/pod-product-compliance
Lightning Source LLC
Chambersburg PA
CBHW070729280626
47159CB00023B/2951